THE PILLARS OF MIDNIGHT

Also by Elleston Trevor and available in the NEL series:

THE SHOOT
THE BILLBOARD MADONNA
THE KILLING GROUND
THE FREEBOOTERS
THE FIRE RAISER
A PLACE FOR THE WICKED

The
Pillars of Midnight

Elleston Trevor

NEW ENGLISH LIBRARY
TIMES MIRROR

First published in Great Britain by William Heinemann Ltd. in 1957
© Elleston Trevor 1957

٭

FIRST NEL EDITION JUNE 1970

٭

NEL Books are published by
New English Library Limited from Barnard's Inn, Holborn, London, E.C.1.
Made and printed in Great Britain by Hunt Barnard & Co. Ltd., Aylesbury, Bucks.

45000519 4

To
Reg and Lily Varney

ONE

On the terrible day of the beginning, Monks woke late and resented it.

'I asked you to get me up early.'

'I just couldn't disturb you, darling. You looked so peaceful, and there's no surgery this morning.'

'There's no surgery for the next two weeks. Are you going to let me oversleep the whole of the holiday?'

Her smile was cool and tender. 'That wouldn't do you any harm either.'

He drank his coffee while she sat by the window writing brief competent notes to the charwoman, the dry-cleaners, the paper-boy, and her sister who was coming tomorrow to look after the house. Her quick pen broke the chains of routine that had governed them both for nearly a year without a break.

'Did they check the car?' They might have forgotten, and he wanted an excuse for his resentment.

'Yes, darling.'

'Will Joanna know where to find the key of the garage, if she wants to get in there?'

'I'm writing to her now.'

The pen moved with annoying competence. Pale sunshine was coming into the window, touching her hair with fair tints as she sat with her head bent, writing. She was too competent, too pretty. He got up. 'I've got to go up to the hospital,' he said. She didn't even turn her head.

'What for, darling?'

'I left the camera there.'

'Do we want to take it with us?'

She folded paper deftly, tucking it into envelopes.

'If you can't use a camera on holiday, when can you?'

'Well, don't hurry. We've got fourteen wonderful days in front of us, and you can take whole albums of photographs.'

He looked down at her as she glanced up, licking an envelope, her tongue pink in the sunshine, her eyes clear. She looked like a child, innocent and impossible. The sour taste of the gum on the envelope made her grimace; then she smiled, turning her head away from him and thumping the flap down, putting the envelope with the others.

Half-way to the hospital, with the clean morning air blowing

7

in at the windows of the car, he realised suddenly that he was starting a holiday and that there was no surgery and that an hour wasted here or there didn't matter. He thought of turning the car round and going back to tell Julie she was pretty, and competent, and faultless in his sight, and that he was just trying to unwind after seven months' rush and worry. But he didn't go back, because she would know these things already, and would laugh at him. Julie knew too much.

The hospital sprawled across the hillside, with the pale sun defining the windows and glinting along the guttering; the wan early light yellowed the oblong of an ambulance that was crawling down the East Road towards the town. It seemed to Monks impossible that he could escape a building as big as this, a routine as strict as his, even for a fortnight; his anxiety returned, and with it fresh resentment. He had left his camera with Preston, who had promised to drop it in at the house, two days ago. Now there was this journey, to fetch it. The building blanked out the sky as he stopped the car in the forecourt; its shadow put the clock back to dawn, and the air was chill.

People were waiting for treatment; some of them said good-morning to him; he smiled, hurrying past, resentful, reminded by the woebegone throng of his routine. Half of them were here because it broke their own routine of washing-up the breakfast things and getting the children off to school, or wandering, retired, from the park to the library and back to the park, their pipes in their thin veined hands, their pensioners' coupons in their dark frayed pockets, and all the day to go before they could sleep and forget that tomorrow would be the same. He was sorrier for them than those who were in honest need of treatment; illness, if you were lucky, was a passing thing.

The camera was not in Preston's locker – his impatience left him no compunction in looking for it there. It was not in the room, anywhere here on the polished tiled window-sill, the bleak white-wood table, the useless chair. Damn Preston! He wasn't going to fish Preston out of his rounds, but he had to find the camera. He stood frustrated, listening to the creak of the central-heating pipes as they cooled slowly after the night's stoke, looking at his watch, thinking of the long road to Cornwall that should have been the longer road to the South of France but Julie had said they couldn't afford it unless they raised an overdraft, and the bank had clamped down anyway, even for emergencies . . . Competent Julie, who knew how they stood and what they could afford to do, and couldn't . . . if only sometimes she could throw her bonnet high over the windmill, and let things – he stopped his thoughts. He was being unfair, even disloyal. Their life would be in a mess if she let him run it, and if she were the impulsive type like Ruth she'd be hell to live with.

He stopped his thoughts again, consciously to realise that so many times when he criticised Julie it was by comparison with Ruth. Ruth's face came into his mind at these times, and her movements, and her sudden laugh – she was there without his thinking of her. He must try not to let it happen, because Julie had more qualities than Ruth could ever dream of, more sweetness and steadiness and gaiety than most women, certainly more than Ruth.

The final thought that flicked through his mind as the door of the room opened was: But is it a question of qualities?

Preston came in and said: 'Hello, Steven . . .'

Monks got rid of the final sneaking thought by answering mentally: Yes, it's a question of qualities. He looked at Preston, who was saying: 'They told me you were here. Is the trip off?'

'Good God no!' There was almost panic in his voice at the thought.

'Then that's all right.' Preston stood awkwardly, hands in the pockets of his white coat. 'As a matter of fact I hoped you might give me five minutes, before you——'

'I came for my camera.'

'Oh.' Preston's glasses caught the light from the window and for a moment Monks couldn't see his eyes. 'Oh – your *camera*.'

'Yes,' Monks said. The man had forgotten, but there was no apology.

'It's in your locker.' The two pale blobs of reflected light from his glasses swept across the wall as he turned his head an inch. 'I'm a bit troubled, as a matter of fact.'

Opening his locker, Monks thought: Whatever it is, he can count me out. Preston was nervous, in the awkward way he stood, in his reliance on the favourite phrase 'as a matter of fact' that Monks knew so well.

'Are you?'

He found the camera and heard Preston say: 'I put it there yesterday. I didn't realise you'd want it.'

If he told Preston he'd promised to drop it at the house it would waste another thirty seconds. Once in the car and on the road with Julie, he'd be all right. Until then, he was trapped.

'That's all right.' He checked the film-indicator. Preston hadn't even used the thing.

'You were out East, in the war,' Preston said.

'Yes.' He slung the camera-strap over one shoulder, looking at Preston, glad that he wouldn't see him for another fortnight.

'I was hoping you'd look at a chap for me.'

'Sorry, Clifford – we've got to get down there before tonight. The hotel's booked.' But Preston was between him and the door. 'Ask Ruddling – he's on the job.'

'But he wasn't out East. I think that's where this thing might

9

have come from, and you're an authority.'

Preston's face was smooth, pink, and troubled. His pale eyes, now visible to Monks in the shadow behind the glasses, were nervously challenging; and Monks resented him, more than he had resented anything else this morning. Because of Preston he was up here at the hospital to fetch his camera; and now, because of Preston, he was going to be kept here——

'Only five minutes, Steve. I'd really appreciate it.'

The central-heating pipes creaked. Someone was wheeling a trolley past the door: the rubber tyres squeaked on the parquet floor, and glass clinked to the vibration. Very calmly Monks asked: 'Who is this chap of yours?'

'Prebble, in Wingfield. You won't have seen him.' Preston turned and opened the door, waiting for him. Monks followed him out, finding a kind of angry patience to control his feelings. In the passage Sister Catteridge passed them.

'Good-morning, Dr. Monks – I thought you were on holiday!'

'So did I.'

They went through the main block to Wingfield Ward. Preston walked slightly ahead of Monks, hurrying a little, his hands still in the pockets of his jacket; it was a pigeon-toed preoccupied walk, the head down an inch, the short steps evenly spaced and automatic, the mind already at the destination, thinking ahead of the body; it was Preston's typical walk, and therefore Monks derided it silently, following the man down the ward until they reached Prebble's bed.

'This one,' Preston murmured, and stood by the bed with his legs slightly apart, his head thrust down to look at Prebble. Behind the bed, one of the windows was wide open and the curtain moved, its hem brushing the sill softly across and across while a bird outside piped suddenly and winged away with its call coming in hurried jerks, diminishing. A loud sound filled the window; men were dumping coke in the stores area, sending up the sound of its rough cascade; and Monks went on looking at the man in the bed and then turned to look at the case-sheet that Sister Gill had brought for him.

'When did he come in?'

'Three days ago, Doctor. On Friday.'

Preston moved past Monks and shut the window, turning back to watch him as he read the report. Charles Ernest Prebble, 49, railway-clerk, had gone to bed with severe frontal headache and pains in the back, four days before being admitted to hospital with an undiagnosed hæmorrhagic rash.

Monks looked down at the man, at the rash.

On the wall, the chart showed ninety-two degrees, falling sharply from Saturday's peak of a hundred and four. Monks looked down again, and pulled the bedclothes back. The man

10

was sweating hard and was watching the two doctors and the sister, his eyes moving every few seconds to switch their scrutiny from one face to another. Then, as Monks opened the pyjama-jacket, Prebble tried to lift his head and look down at himself. Monks said:

'Don't worry. You're properly peppered.'

He let Sister Gill fix the pyjamas and pull the bedclothes up while he read the case-sheet for the second time; and while he read it his mind became suddenly filled with a rush of images. Vaguely he realised that Preston was watching him, waiting for him to speak. At one instant he found himself staring over the edge of the case-sheet at the bobbing bow at the back of Sister Gill's uniform as she moved about. Wondering why there was no sound from outside the building, he looked up and saw that someone had shut the window. Aware of a weight dragging at one shoulder he put his hand up, and found the camera-strap, and swung it off his arm, putting it on the floor by the bed cabinet. There were flowers on the cabinet; daffodils for Prebble; somebody loved him.

'Have you ever been in contact with anyone from the east of Suez?'

Monks was aware of Preston's head swinging up to look at him. Prebble was trying to talk but there was phlegm in his throat and he cleared it laboriously. It wasn't a difficult question.

'My lad,' he said.

'What?'

'My boy. On the India run.' His voice was peaceful; he was proud of his lad. Monks bent lower.

'What does your boy do?'

'Steward. Home on leave. He's not sick, Doc.'

'Good. A steward in a ship?'

'Oh no. Air service. BEC Lines. He's all right.'

The sheet reported the last use of opium ten hours ago. Monks said slowly: 'When did your son arrive home?'

'I don't remember. On leave, Doc. What's the matter with me?'

'You're all right. Can't you remember when your lad came home?'

'He's on leave. Am I bad, Doc? Am I?'

'Not very.'

Sister Gill said from behind Monks' shoulder: 'He's been talking a great deal about his son. I think the boy's been home for a good fortnight, Doctor.'

'The India run,' said Prebble, and started shivering.

Monks looked down at him. There was going to be so much to do, while this man died.

'I'm cold,' Prebble said.

11

Monks moved, kicked against something, looked down, saw it was his camera, picked it up, looked at Preston and said:

'Good. Who's next?' When they were out of Prebble's hearing he said: 'Matron's office.' Preston walked quickly beside him.

'What do you think it is?'

'Have you taken a blood-test?'

'I had a sample sent to Colindale. We're waiting to hear from them. What do you think it is?'

A nurse was helping a boy along the corridor; he was stumping along, hissing his breath in every time his left foot came down. When they had gone past, Monks said:

'I think it's smallpox.'

Preston dropped back and Monks stopped, turning to look at him. He was standing still, in the middle of the corridor, looking at Monks. His narrow preoccupied head had gone down and his eyes looked steadily up at Monks as if he suddenly suspected him of a crime. His hands were dug into the pockets of his white coat and did not move. The odd thought in Monks' head was that if Preston ever became famous and had a monument, it would be like this. It would have this marble stillness.

'Are you sure?' Preston sounded slightly impatient.

'No. I said I think it is. We'd better phone Colindale, and see Matron.'

He walked on, and in a moment Preston's crêpe soles came squeaking up behind him. 'I've never been in this kind of situation, Steven. What's the most important thing to do?'

'Prevent panic,' Monks said.

On the telephone, Julie asked: What's it about, darling?'

'Just a delay,' Monks said. 'A couple of hours. Then we'll be on the road.'

'All right. Tell me when you get back.'

'Yes.' He put the telephone down as a nurse looked in at the door.

'We're ready for you, Doctor.'

She was very young, and looked over-confident. How would she take it when they asked her to volunteer to stay? He tied his dressing-gown cord more neatly and followed her along the passage to the disinfection unit, where they were already doing his clothes.

Matron had given an exaggerated shrug when Preston had explained.

'These things are sent to try us,' she had said. Monks couldn't think of a better reaction. She had called up the M.O. and he had come down to her office; and Monks had left the two of them arguing whether they should wait for the report from Colindale or call the Kingsbourne M.O.H. first. Preston had asked him, outside, what he should do about Ruth.

'Why? Where is she?'

'In London. She's coming back this afternoon.'

'Then phone her. Tell her to get herself vaccinated before she gets on the train, and don't forget she's the type to dismiss the idea of a smallpox epidemic with a light laugh. Tell her that if she comes home without a scratch on her arm she'll have to be isolated for the next fourteen days.'

Preston had frowned. 'It won't mean that, will it?'

'No, but it's the worst threat you can give her. You know that.'

'Yes, I see.' But there was no conviction. He had been thinking about Prebble, not Ruth.

Monks stood in the disinfection unit, sick of the smell of formalin, and thought about Prebble, and the look on Ruddling's face when Matron had told him, and Ruth's arm with her sleeve rolled up, and the road to Cornwall.

They gave him a clean dressing-gown and he put it on, to wait until his clothes were ready. Outside the tiny room people seemed to be walking more quickly and voices were quieter than usual; or did he imagine it? They wouldn't have been told, yet, or shouldn't have been. Listening to the footsteps and the voices outside, he reminded himself that he was dissociated from it all, for two weeks. If they could stamp this thing out in two weeks, the quarantine period would be over, and he would be back from his holiday to the normal routine.

But they'd be lucky. He had worked it out before he had left Wingfield Ward, where Charles Ernest Prebble lay dying. Three days here, four days in bed, following the incubation period of eleven days or so. Eighteen days. Call it twenty, to be safe. The disease had been in the town for twenty days already.

It had been brought in by the boy. A steward, with BEC. On the India run. Prebble would die proud of his son.

Julie sat with her left arm along the window, which was down. The soft rush of air was mild now, because the sun had strengthened towards noon. They took the short road out of Kingsbourne, cutting down by the park and through the railway arch below the station.

'Where did you stow the camera, Steven?'

The sunshine was cut off by the archway; then the road was bright again.

'I didn't bring it. I forgot about it.' He gave a rueful laugh that didn't quite come off.

'Tell me what's happened, up there.'

'At the hospital?'

'Yes. It made you forget your precious camera.'

The shadow of leaves mottled the road and rushed dark across the cellulose of bonnet and wings. It was a perfect motoring day,

13

and made him sharply conscious of life.

'They've got a chap there with suspected smallpox. I didn't tell you, on the phone, because someone there might have overheard me, and started a panic before they were told in the proper way.' He felt uneasily that his voice had trailed off.

It was some time before she answered; he could see in the outer field of his vision that she had turned her head to look at him. 'How long has he had it?'

It was no good lying to Julie. 'He's in the last stages now.'

Her voice was ominously level. 'Did you examine him?'

'I had a look at him. Clifford asked me to. It's his patient.'

'You touched him, then.'

'Yes. Don't worry, I went through the bug-morgue before I came away, clothes and everything.'

She lifted her hand and he felt her stroking his left arm, just below the shoulder. 'Oh darling, you're such a damn' fool, sometimes,' she said. 'You know we can't leave, now.'

Without meaning to, he moved his foot down on the throttle another degree. He said: 'I'm perfectly safe. So are you. I've been disinfected completely, and you've just felt the lint on my arm. Don't tell me you want us to chuck up our trip just because there's a bit of panic on?'

She put her hands on the windscreen, fingers spread, as she worked out the situation, asking him the few vital questions and knowing he wouldn't lie. In the end she said: 'So it's been in the town nearly three weeks.'

'Not infectiously. The man's rash only began four days ago, and he was taken straight into hospital——'

'Darling, let's be quite honest – and it's not often I have to say that to you. It's his boy who's been the danger in the town. He's a carrier. For three weeks. This isn't just an isolated case – it's the start of an outbreak.'

The road wound round small hills. There was no enjoyment now in watching the play of sun and shadow. 'All right,' he said, 'it's an outbreak. So?'

'I'm going back.'

Evenly he asked: 'Why?'

'Because I can help.'

'How?'

'They might call for volunteer nurses, and I'm still qualified.'

'Don't you feel you've earned a break, Julie?'

'Yes. Much less than you. But I couldn't begin to enjoy myself, away.'

'You feel you're dedicated to crisis, by birth? It has some fascination for you?'

She was nice enough to touch his arm, this time to attempt contact with him. 'We could talk all day, and nothing would

14

change my mind. I'm not dedicated, just obstinate. You've worked like a black for months, Steven, so you can just put me down anywhere here, and I'll get a lift back into Kingsbourne——'

'But for God's sake, you——'

'No, please, Steven. I shan't spoil your holiday. A woman's no good on a river-bank with a fly-rod, anyway; you'll have perfect peace and find some wonderful friends if you feel you need company.'

He pulled the car into the roadside. They were five miles out of Kingsbourne, already in deep country under spring sunlight, with the rods stowed in the back and new gaudy flies to be bought in the small quiet shops of Cornish villages . . . new beds to sleep in and new windows in the mornings, with trees and birds they'd never seen before, voices they'd never heard along the streets outside. He said:

'You owe it to me, this holiday.' He meant it.

She realised she could end the argument, with that one word.

'All right, darling. If it's a question of "owing", then I'll come.'

Driving more slowly back, after they had turned the car round in a farm gateway, they found the sun in their eyes, and pulled the shields down to leave half their faces in shadow.

'You should have married someone outside your own profession, Steve. Someone who wouldn't know about these things.'

'I just felt like a break.'

'I know. You can still have one, without me. I do wish you would.'

They had been married for eleven years, so that he could say, more easily than a younger husband could have said: 'It wouldn't be the same.'

When they reached their house in Rutland Square, Steven telephoned the hospital to find out what was happening, and was put through to the matron. She told him in a rather impatient voice:

'Colindale confirms smallpox, Doctor Monks. We've had a second case brought in and the hospital has been put under immediate quarantine. The M.O.H. is circulating all general practitioners, and they'll be able to give you more information at his office.'

'Who is the other case?'

'A young girl, Miss Williams.'

'Where does she work?'

'At the Royalty. An usherette.'

He thanked her and rang off. The room was silent, deep at the back of the house. A railway-clerk, and now a cinema usherette. The Royalty was on the far side of the town from the railway station, three miles away. It was a long path for the virus to take,

15

through a hundred and fifty thousand people.

He heard Julie coming into the room. Her slight shadow flickered across the sunlight on the floor. 'What do they say, Steven?'

'It's spreading.'

TWO

Buckridge stood in the middle of a vague circle of men, some of them with coats on, holding their hats, others in their clerical suits or sports-jackets, their ties negative-green and their pullovers negative-brown; most had pens clipped into the breast-pocket of their jackets and the metal enamelled badge of some club or other in their lapels Most of their shoes were black, and few polished; there were wrinkles in their socks. But their hair was neat and their faces pink, except for the older men of the older school – the traditional Civil Servant fighting a rearguard against the sports-coats and crêpe soles.

Most of them were smoking, a few of them small pipes with flattened-looking bowls. Spectacles glinted among the rows of faces, catching the shine of the late-afternoon sun. No one was talking, now. They looked at one another and sometimes at the Chief Sanitary Inspector, Buckridge.

Buckridge was a thin stumpy man with a hard straight body, clear Celtic eyes and great grey eyebrows that dominated his gaze: talking to him, one's eyes were drawn upwards, hypnotically, to study those shaggy brows. They were much more impressive than a moustache, and not only because there were two of them. The top of an expensive-looking fountain-pen glinted above his breast-pocket: that would be a present from the wife. Everything he carried about with him was a present from the wife – his wrist-watch, tie-pin, cigarette-lighter, cuff-links – 'a little thing the wife gave me'. This phrase, known well to his older colleagues and staff, summed up his marriage. This thin, hard, disciplined man was adored by his wife, and these were her gifts to show the world. He was proud of them, proud of her, and just a shade bewildered. He didn't, he thought, deserve it.

He looked at the men about him. None of them knew, yet. The few people who had been told were already out there in the town, working against the enemy. These men here were reinforcements. They didn't look much of an army.

'I shan't keep you long.'

Their faces turned towards him. A hand crushed a cigarette out in the ash-tray on his desk. A spectacle-case snapped shut with the sound of a small bomb going off. A lighter clicked. The noise of traffic drummed against the closed windows, bringing a sense of isolation to this high, close room.

'What I want to tell you is that we've got a case of smallpox in the town.'

A double-decker thundered by, going through Market Square; a pane of glass vibrated, buzzing. The few words echoed in their heads.

'Some of you may not know what that means, but it won't take me long to tell you. Smallpox – this type that's been discovered – is a killer. Unless there's been vaccination, the death-rate among the people who catch it is something in the region of seventy per cent.' He began watching them in turn. One or two of them had been out East, he knew. They didn't want any telling. But some were young enough to have complete faith in the tidal wave of new experimental drugs from America. They were the dangerous people, who wouldn't take it seriously until it was too late. 'This first case is up at King's Hospital. He's pretty bad. There's a second case, but we don't know whether it's dangerous or modified. What we do know is that there'll be others. Smallpox is caused by a bug – a virus. It's contagious and infectious. It's been in this town for three weeks, maybe longer.'

Somebody murmured, 'Christ! . . .' Buckridge swung his head.

'Yes. We shall need His help.'

Their faces had changed, much or little. They were forgetting the cigarettes in their fingers. They didn't hear the next bus that went by, though it vibrated the window-pane. Their eyes spoke to him, particularly those of the men whom he knew well.

Come off it, Bucky, you're out to scare us.

Who's slipped up? Why didn't they find it earlier?

Smallpox. . . . I'd sooner see rats on the march.

Bang goes my bloody leave.

They watched the Chief Sanitary Inspector point to the wall map of Kingsbourne. 'The first case worked at the railway station as a clerk, though he didn't come into touch with the public, fortunately.' He moved his thin, strong hand across the map. 'The second case worked at the cinema, here. That is the path of the disease.' He dropped his hand. 'By now, there'll be side-lanes. We have the original carrier, who came into the town from India three weeks ago, still with us. How many people does a person come into contact with in three weeks? It depends. A good few hundred, perhaps a thousand. We can safely say,' he went on more quietly, his brows swinging like short, soft antlers as he looked at them in turn, 'that there are at the very least a thousand people in this town at risk. They will be the people who have come into touch with the carrier, with the first case, or the second case. Our job is to find those people, warn them, examine them, vaccinate them and isolate them for sixteen days.'

Involuntarily one of them said: 'They won't stand for it.'

Buckridge swung his head. He gazed in silence at the man who had spoken until he was looking back at him. Then Buckridge answered him carefully, speaking as if to a child, taking great care with the pronounciation of the last word.

'This is a plague.'

His gaze was bird-like, bright and unwinking. When he seemed satisfied that his message was made clear, he spoke more briskly. 'On the medical and general administration side, action has already been taken. The local public health laboratory has been asked to build up lymph stocks. Air-crew and passengers of the carrier's aeroplane are being traced and dealt with, together with the entire ground-staff of London Airport. The Kingsbourne head postmaster has been notified of the outbreak and a circular has gone out to all medical practitioners. The staff and patients at the hospital have been vaccinated and the hospital put under quarantine. Downstairs, in this building, there are two pretty nurses waiting for you when you leave here, and they want you with jackets off and the left sleeve rolled up.'

A ragged laugh rose. Suddenly they saw themselves as a herd of sheep waiting for the sheep-dip. The idea relieved them; as Buckridge had talked, each of them had begun slowly to realise his own individual responsibility in the face of this crisis; but now he could go with the herd. Their laughter died away.

'I don't hold with vaccination,' a young man said. Buckridge flicked him a glance.

'You conscientiously object to being vaccinated, Cleaver?'

'Yes, sir. Even in the Army, I did.'

'Very well. You'll please leave here within ten minutes for sixteen days' special leave. I'll arrange it for you.'

In the new gust of laughter there was disbelief. Was that all you had to say? You objected? Sixteen days!

Cleaver himself was shaken, suspecting a catch. He asked:

'On pay, sir?'

'On full pay,' said Buckridge. He paused for three seconds. 'It'll be encouraging for us to think of you sitting by the fire with a book, when we're working twelve hours a day. If we think of you at all.'

The telephone on Buckridge's desk began ringing and he answered it, and said: 'They're coming down now.' When he had put the receiver down he said to them: 'I'd like sanitary inspectors and their assistants to report back to me in half an hour. Your job will be to trace all contacts and throw a barrier of vaccination across the path of the disease. I shall tell you how we plan to do that.'

Early in the afternoon, Monks had gone with the Kingsbourne Medical Officer of Health in his official car to visit Prebble's house. A mobile disinfectant unit followed them, a dark green

19

van with shining sides and the Council crest. They worked their way through thick afternoon traffic to the crowded part of the town near the station.

Monks had had a good lunch, beautifully prepared by Julie; it would be their last civilised meal for some time. He sat listening to Tewson, who drove with impatience.

'We've dealt with Prebble's boy, the carrier. He's been disinfected and asked to stay in the town at our disposal. The Ministry's asked the BBC to broadcast an appeal to all visitors to the hospital here since Prebble's reception – and incidentally I've caught a rap on the knuckles for not phoning the Ministry the moment I was told that smallpox was suspected, after your diagnosis.'

'When was the Ministry told?'

'Not long after. We had Colindale phone them direct, to save time, when the diagnosis was confirmed.' He braked hard behind a bus pulling out. Monks said:

'Official toes are tender, this year.'

'Oh, they've got a point. The Minister requests immediate information on suspicion, not confirmation. Not that he could take any action.' He sat squarely at the wheel, a biggish man, his shoulders hunched over the wheel as if he were lifting the car along. 'Where's that van gone?' His mirror was blank. Monks turned round.

'Taken a short cut.'

'I told them to follow us.' He swung into a side-road with a slight squeal of tyres. 'It's left, here, isn't it?'

'No. Right.'

'They know the way better than I do. I spend too much time in my office. I'm sorry about your leave.'

'There are worse troubles, in this town.'

Monks' thought-train took him at once to Prebble, lying in the iron-framed bed, with stubble sprouting through the rash; from Prebble to Sister Gill and then Preston, standing looking down, worried, waiting – and then Ruth, because she was Preston's wife. Ruth in London. He had asked Preston, on the telephone:

'Did you tell Ruth?'

'I told her friend. Ruth was out shopping.'

Later, just before Monks had left the house to meet the M.O.H., Preston had telephoned him, with some strange late conscience about the camera. He must have remembered, in a moment of calm, that he had promised to drop it in at the house.

'I've had it disinfected. Will you pick it up, Steven?'

'I can't, without going through the bug-morgue all over again; besides, there's nothing to take pictures of except the queues at the clinics.'

Before he had rung off, Preston had said: 'Ruth isn't coming

20

home until it's all over.'

'Did she phone you?'

'I got a message through the hospital.' Preston seemed to be waiting for a comment, and Steven said:

'Well, you wouldn't have much time for her, in the next week or so.'

'No.' And Clifford had rung off without talking any more about Ruth.

Steven got her out of his mind, hearing Tewson say:

'This is the street.'

A poor street, with narrow pavements where children sat writing with chalk. The railings were dark with age and weather and neglect outside each house, and dirt was on the basement windows as thick as scum on a pond. From the other end of the street came the green van, stopping outside Number 17. A police-car was already parked there, being stared at by women and children and a few old men with nothing to do.

Tewson pulled up and said: 'How many of these people would crowd round an unexploded bomb?'

'All of them.'

Steven got his bag and went into the house with him. The people fell away for them, then closed in, satisfied that they were missing nothing.

The front room was bright with cheap new furniture and china ornaments; the television set dominated the scene, its shiny top bare of knick-knacks, its shiny sides well clear of the adjoining furniture, that left respectful room for the easy-payment shrine. There was the smell of chimney soot and peppermints.

'Is there any change, Doctor?'

A thin woman, once pretty, now tired, the mother of too many children, the scrubber of too many steps, her fair hair recently permed: that would have been to see her husband at the hospital, Steven thought.

'We can't expect much change, Mrs. Prebble.'

She looked already a widow.

'I see.'

She didn't really see; she accepted.

'Have you been told what all this is about?' Tewson asked her. Steven thought his voice was extraordinarily gentle, more than he had ever heard it before.

'The p'licemen have told us,' she said. 'It's very bad.'

'It could be worse. Things can always be worse. You understand how you can help us, then, by staying in your house for a couple of weeks, and taking it easy.'

'Yes, Doctor.' She accepted this, too. She didn't accept whatever came to her in life, but these people were officials, and it was their job to know what was right.

21

'I'd like to start work,' murmured Steven, and Tewson said to Mrs. Prebble:

'Dr. Monks wants to make a brief check-up, if he may. All the people who live here. It won't take long.'

She showed them to another, smaller room, and three children shuffled back to give them space. Two boys, sixteen-year-olds, and a younger girl. Tewson came back to the front room while Steven began work.

One of the patrol-car crew had come in from the street, having seen the M.O.H. arrive. 'I've got all you asked for, sir.' Tewson looked at the list; there were sixteen names and addresses of people who had called at this house during the last eleven days, among them the milkman, postman, newspaper-boy, insurance-agent and rent-collector.

'Use your radio, will you? Get the operations-room to telephone this list to the Chief Sanitary Inspector's office. He'll take over from there.'

'Right, sir. And shall we stand-by, after that?'

'Unless you get a call.'

As the constable turned to go out Tewson said: 'And look to those people outside, will you? Get all their names and where they live in this street, and ask them to be kind enough to go home and wait for us to visit them. I think you'll have a job on.'

The constable grinned gently. 'Oh no, sir. I live in this street myself.' He went away. Tewson thought: That'll be the house near the end with the clean windows and blue front-door. He said to Mrs. Prebble, who was quietly pulling the hearth-rug a few inches to cover a stain on the floor:

'You won't have to worry about groceries and things, Mrs. Prebble. Everything you need will be delivered – but you mustn't answer the door to anyone except the sanitary inspectors and their men. We'll put a special bin outside where your supplies will keep clean and dry till you fetch them in.'

'I see, Doctor, yes.'

'I'm sorry, but we don't want you to write any letters. You see, although you and your family are being protected by vaccination and regular inspection, there might be a germ or two left hanging about, and they can be carried by a letter. You might be sending a bad illness through the post to your best friends and relations. That's very important, isn't it?'

'I was on welfare work in the war,' she said, and he knew that she meant she could be relied on as a responsible person.

'Well that's a relief to me,' he said. 'It's people like you that we need to help us.'

He turned as one of the boys came in from the passage with a tray of tea. She moved to help him. Tewson said: 'When the inspectors come round to see you, every day, they'll bring news of your husband, so that you won't really be out of touch.'

'I see,' she said, and balanced the tray on the table by the wall. 'You'll have a cup of tea, Doctor?' She hadn't been listening, even to the mention of her husband. She was worried about the china – was it all clean, none of the cups cracked? Tewson looked at the tray and the gleaming cups with their invisible lethal dose of variola bacteria.

'It's very kind of you, but I've so many calls to make.' He had been vaccinated at the hospital this morning, but it might not have taken. 'I didn't know you were going to such trouble.'

Steven came out of the back room with a handful of broken thermometers wrapped in brown paper.

'Examined and vaccinated,' he said, and saw the tray. 'And all ready for tea.'

'Then we'll be off.' Tewson looked at Mrs. Prebble. 'I know you won't forget the things I've told you. You realise how important it is. If everyone else does the same, we'll put paid to this business in no time.'

When he had gone out of the house with Steven, Mrs. Prebble looked down at the tray with its steaming teapot and six cups and saucers. Everything matched. The other boy and the girl came from the back room, the boy slipping his jacket on. The girl said: 'Why didn't they want any tea, Mum?'

She didn't answer, but looked at the boy. 'What did he say, about Dad?'

'No change.' He was the man of the house. He had to keep the women cheerful. '*He'll* be okay, don't worry.'

His mother was trying to remember. 'No, he said something about people bringing us any news.'

'The inspectors, he said.'

The girl leaned her arms along the mantelpiece, her thin body sagging suddenly. She spoke with her mouth against the crook of her arm. 'I'm frightened.'

The others turned on her.

'Frightened?'

'What for, Daph?'

'We got no need to be frightened – look at the trouble they're takin'!'

Her mother went up to the girl, holding her round the waist. It was a thin waist; Daphne had never eaten much, and never put on proper weight. If there were colds about, Daph always got them; and there was that time they'd all had with her when she'd been taken with a fever, and nobody knew for certain what it was. 'You should get her to take more nourishment, Mrs. Prebble, or she'll have no resistance to fight these things.'

Her waist was so thin, and the slight body was shaking now as she began crying quietly. The boys felt embarrassed and the elder one, the man of the house, said: 'Now then, Daph, no water-works, eh?'

There was just the sound of her sniffing, and the bleak tick of the clock. Mrs. Prebble drew her daughter away from the mantelpiece, with the mark of its hard edge across her arms. 'What we want is a cup o' tea, that's all. You can start pourin' out, Sidney.'

They gathered round the tray, intent upon the ritual of pouring out and handing round, while the clock ticked and someone's face peered in at them from the window, then went away.

The woman's voice was quiet in the room; she picked her way through words that mustn't be said, that might frighten Daphne. 'If anyone comes to the door, Sidney, we mustn't answer it, till we're told. Not for two weeks. And none of us can't go out.'

'Okay,' he said. 'First one tryin' to skip off gets a wallop across the backside.' But the others didn't laugh. He stirred his tea, and said in a moment: 'I'll tell you what. I'll get the cards out, an' we'll all 'ave a game of rummy. Eh?'

His mother sat on the arm of the chair where Daphne was sitting with her untouched tea.

'Yes,' she said gently. 'We'll have a lot of games.'

Mr. Buckridge looked round with a sharp swing of his head. 'Where's Collins?'

'Coming,' one of them said.

'Get him in here. Time's short.' He went on sharpening the pencil. It had a gold-coloured top, to match the pen, and he prized it.

Footsteps came up the stairs outside. Someone hissed – 'Come on, Bert, we're all waiting for you!'

The telephone rang and Buckridge answered it with an alert pounce of his hand. 'Buckridge here.'

'Police here, Mr. Buckridge – "A" Division operations. We've got a list of contacts for you.'

Buckridge told him to hold on, switched the call through to the administration room below, told them to make fifteen copies of the list and send it in to him, and put the receiver down, looking up at Collins. 'Door, please.'

Someone closed it.

'You may smoke and make yourselves comfortable.' His penknife scraped neatly at the graphite, and he blew the dust away, putting the pencil down beside the six others. 'First of all, you should know that the medical side of this operation is running at top speed. All public servants – police, emergency services, postal staffs and ourselves – have now been vaccinated. In four days from now – that's on Friday – we'll be inspected to make sure the vaccine has taken, but from today we're protected enough to be guaranteed immunity in the general duties we'll be engaged on.' His head swung slowly to look at his fifteen inspectors. 'So we're safe.'

Cigarette smoke was thickening among them. One of them was carefully scraping the dottle from his pipe, but looking up at Mr. Buckridge to show he was attending. Bucky could cut up very rough, when he liked; and there was a crisis on.

'You've all got a general idea about smallpox. Our main job is to trace contacts. It's detective-work.' He paused, and spoke more slowly. 'A contact of a case of smallpox, even if he's already infected, doesn't infect anyone else until the first symptoms show up, some time after the tenth day. Until the tenth day, he's not a danger. All we have to do is report his name as soon as we find him, and leave him to the doctors. They'll vaccinate him and isolate him in his house or wherever he is, for sixteen days. The welfare people will look after his needs. If the disease develops, he won't have infected anyone. Is that clear?'

They nodded, shuffled.

'Ten days,' someone said.

Buckridge fingered his array of pencils. 'We've got a team of six doctors working alongside us, more or less in liaison – but we've got two different jobs to do. Let them do theirs, and they won't get in our way. Your job is to visit all the contacts on your individual lists, warn them of their position, and tell them to go to their doctor for immediate vaccination. When you find a contact is ill, or even complaining of a sore throat, you report him to this office at once by telephone, and we'll send a doctor from the team. At the same time, you must get all the information possible from the contact regarding his movements during the last few days. Your doctor on the spot will tell you how many days are significant, according to what stage of sickness the contact is in. You must also get a list of names from him: the names of all those people he's been in contact with during the the days in question. If possible, telephone the list to me. We shall break it up and add the names to the quota of contacts to be visited, warned, vaccinated and kept under surveillance. There's more to tell you, but at this point I'd like questions.'

He had no time to turn his head and look at Collins before Collins said: 'Are our own families being vaccinated, sir?'

'They are. It's essential.'

'This surveillance,' said Thompson. 'How does it go?'

'Every day,' Buckridge said, 'we shall, between us, visit every contact.'

'*Every* contact.'

'Yes. By this evening we shall have upwards of a thousand contacts of the original carrier – who was infectious for three weeks – and of the two smallpox cases at the hospital, who were

25

infectious at the onset of their symptoms after the ten-day incubation-period.'

Someone asked: 'These are primary contacts, sir. What about secondaries?'

'To be warned, vaccinated, and told to report to a doctor at the slightest sign of an illness, even a sore throat or backache.'

'No daily surveillance.'

'No.'

A bus went by, vibrating the window-pane. When the sound had stopped, Buckridge asked: 'Any more questions?'

'What powers have we, sir?'

Buckridge's head swung. 'The power of persuasion.'

'What about awkward customers?'

'Telephone me. But not until after you've tried tact, friendliness, patience. A lot of these people will be frightened.'

'What do we do when we've finished our list?'

'Bring it in. We'll give you another one.' His hand was on the telephone before its second ring. 'Buckridge,' he said, and listened. They watched him, and saw his face tighten. With the receiver in his hand he swung the chair round, and looked up at the map on the wall.

THREE

In the evening of the third day there was a fine drizzle falling over
the town. Through it, black cars moved. People stood with
umbrellas in lengthening lines outside the two main vaccination
clinics that had been set up to ease the burden on doctors'
surgeries, where contacts had queued for hours before being told
that lymph stocks were exhausted and that delivery would be
from London and therefore delayed. Anxiety was spreading. It
was quelled from time to time by the two teams who were on the
move constantly in their cars, the sanitary inspectors and the
doctors: but rumours sprang up in different parts of the town and
had to run their course.

In the afternoon, Charles Prebble had died. A nurse had come
to Dr. Preston, saying simply: 'He's dead.' Preston had nodded,
saying nothing as he went with the nurse along the corridors, his
walk automatic and preoccupied. He had known Prebble would
die. His resistance had withdrawn, yesterday, beyond the point
where he could have begun fighting back. This announcement
was a formality. Immediate cremation had been arranged for.

The hospital was quiet, not because Prebble had died – people
had died here before – but because after two days' bewildering
activity there was now a sudden release of tension. The system
was running, and there was a moment for the staff to realise what
it would mean to be imprisoned in this great building for sixteen
days, or longer.

In Wingfield Ward they had heard about Prebble, the man in
the isolation room. They watched Dr. Preston going through and
into the corridor. Their voices were quiet.

'He's gone, then.'

The doors swung shut after the bobbing nurse.

'Bound to, wasn't he?'

Somewhere a telephone was ringing but nobody answered it.

'They done all they could.'

A man stared up at the ceiling, his pinched face tilted, his red
eyes tracing a line on the ceiling where the paper joined, tracing
it back. The thin hair-line began nowhere and ended nowhere;
he could only see part of it. He said to no one:

'They don't care.'

The telephone went on ringing. It got on their nerves.

'I wouldn't want their job, then.'

27

The telephone stopped ringing.

Dr. Preston came back, hands in the pockets of his white jacket. Their heads turned slowly to watch him; then the doors swung shut.

A nurse stood at a window in the long polished corridor, looking out, her hands together on the polished sill. She turned away when she heard Dr. Preston coming. He did not notice her. There had been no phone-call from Ruth today. For most of the day he was able to forget her. He should be glad she wasn't there in the town, exposed to risk. He tried to be glad, walking along with his head down, going past the matron's room, remembering, turning back. She had asked to see him, when he had time. Matron was working very hard. He had told her: 'You're not sleeping enough.'

She had looked at him critically.

'You should be a good judge of that, Doctor Preston.'

He knocked on her door and went in.

The nurse came back to her window, and looked out again. A blue van was unloading at the doors of the empty garage by the East Road. Supplies were being dropped for the two hundred people in the building. Doris, taking over her place on the night-shift, had said: 'How do you spell "siege"?'

The nurse's hands were cold on the polished windowsill. The glass was cold against her brow as she leaned forward. This far she could escape. A man with a flat trolley was trundling down the East Road towards the garage, where the stores had been piled. Another man followed him.

She spoke aloud, her breath clouding on the glass. 'We're untouchables.'

Her arm itched. She mustn't scratch it.

The girl in the isloation ward was a gay little thing, with bad feet. 'This way to the one-and-ninepennies,' she always said when someone went near her bed.

The sill was cold; she took her hands away. The stiff collar chafed her neck and her arm itched under the dressing. Last night she'd been sick, and had no supper. She'd been silly to go and volunteer. Doris had said: 'We're all daft, the lot of us.'

The two men were wheeling their trollies back, pushing them slowly up the drive, calling to each other. A box dropped off and they both stopped.

The light was grey in the tall window. They said it was going to rain.

In the evening, the rain brightened the pavements where the people stood, some of them reading the paper under their umbrellas. There was a short statement from the Medical Officer of Health:

'To date, three cases of smallpox have occurred in Kingsbourne and they have been removed to hospital. Various suspect cases outside the hospital are under close observation. Contacts of confirmed and suspected cases have been vaccinated. Anyone who thinks that he or she is a contact of these cases should go to their doctor and request immediate vaccination, which is of course free and is quickly done. There are ample supplies of vaccine now available to all doctors and the two emergency clinics. All possible steps have been taken to combat the outbreak, and all services are working well. It is hoped that by this early action the spread of the disease will be restricted and soon arrested.'

Drips fell from the tips of the umbrella-spokes, gathering in miniature brilliants and trembling for an instant against the lamplight, then falling away. The big tyres of buses hissed over the wet street. The queue wound into the clinic, into the smell of damp mackintoshes and disinfectant. The people going in watched the people coming out. Had it hurt?

'How long have you been here, mate?'

'Me? Half-hour.'

'Tch!'

A child was crying. It had never seen so many people, except outside the pictures on a Saturday night, and people outside the pictures weren't like this. Everyone was so quiet and serious and grown-up-looking.

'What's happening, Mummy?'

'Nothing, darling.'

A man said: 'That's true enough. Pity we can't get a cup of tea somewhere.'

'You'd think they'd have it organised.'

The people who were to be next said nothing. Their heads were dodging slowly from one side to the other as they peered over the shoulders in front of them. Sometimes they could catch a glimpse of a nurse's cap. The smell of disinfectant was strong in here now. Not unpleasant. It was a reassuring smell. It was a smell against disease.

'I can't wait any longer. I've got my husband coming home for his supper.'

'Take my place, lady. Here y'are.'

Their feet shuffled.

'I wouldn't think of it. It's a perfect disgrace. And they tell us that everything's working well!' She went away.

'It was nice of you, that.' A very small man in big glasses, looking mildly up into the next man's face.

'Eh?'

'To offer the lady.'

'Oh. Ne' mind, she's independent.' They turned their heads.

29

She had come back. She said:

'I never thanked you. I was so annoyed, waiting all this time. It was most kind of you – *most* kind.'

'You're welcome, lady.' He watched the long feather bobbing on her hat. It went whisking away again.

'Somebody's passin' out, mate.'

'Eh?'

'Who?'

'Where?'

They craned their necks. He said drily: 'It's me. For the want of a cupper tea.'

One of them laughed.

The man who was next said nothing. They were doing a boy of about eleven with a ginger head and pale eyes, one sock down and his pockets bulging. He held his jacket over his right arm.

'That's it, old chap. Off you go. Don't take the dressing off until Friday.'

Their feet shuffled. The man who was next tried not to go forward. His mouth was dry.

'Coat off, please. Left sleeve up.'

They nudged him forward. The girl helped him off with his coat. He looked odd. 'It won't take a minute. Right up, please.'

He thought: A boy not much older than Henry. If he can do it, I can do it.

'You've had no vaccination before?'

The nurse was cleaning his arm. The cotton swab felt freezing. 'No. Never.'

He tried to see what they were doing. The nurse had fair hair and grey eyes, and seemed very competent. She made him turn his head straight by putting her left hand on his shoulder from the front, working with her right. Her bright hair under the cap was all he could see. The room closed in on him as he felt the needle at work. The air had gone cold and the lights dim. Her hair shone faintly. The room gathered against him and voices came eerily.

'Mrs. Monks——'

'Yes?'

'I think he's feeling . . .'

Darkness burst against his head.

Julie caught his arm and her assistant steadied him.

'Keep him upright – let me finish him – we shan't get him in here again.' The vaccine mingled with the blood, yellow and crimson. 'Dressing.'

He was quite a weight, for a small man. His head lolled.

'Give me a hand here, please.'

They got him to a chair and someone fetched a glass of water. The feet shuffled.

'Sleeve right up, please. That's it.'

'What was up with 'im, Miss?'

'Felt a little faint. Hold steady now.'

'Think if I come over faint you'd throw your arms roun' me like you did with 'im?'

'At any other time it would be a pleasure, but we're a fraction busy now.'

'That's me. Always the right question at the wrong time. Ne' mind.'

He gave a rich wink and pulled his sleeve down. He smelled of cheap tobacco, sweat and coal-dust, and had the face of a dissolute emperor. Julie smiled to him as he went.

'There's a cup of tea for you when you're ready, Mrs. Monks.'

'Give me another half an hour, then you can take over. Steady, please.'

She was sick of the sight of lymph and blood, of the smell in here, of the serious scared faces, the funny remarks. Her feet were numb. She was hungry. Her hands alone worked perfectly, moving with a deft rhythm arrived at through repetition. She felt that if she went to sleep on her feet, these hands would continue to do these things.

'What's the time, somebody?'

'Mary!'

'M'm?'

'Got the time?'

'Quarter past.'

'Quarter past what?'

'Nine.'

'Quarter past nine, Mrs. Monks.'

'Is Mrs. Morris here yet?'

'I think so.'

'Make sure, please.'

'Yes, she's here.'

'Then Mary can go off. Ask her to change the bin before she leaves.'

'Yes, Mrs. Monks.'

'Thank you. Don't take the dressing off until Friday. Have you given them your name and address?'

'Yes, Miss.'

The feet shuffled. The closed umbrellas had made a small pool in the corner. Someone had left his behind; it fell over like a black dead bird.

'Steady, please. Hold still.'

Faintly from the street came a paper-seller's shout.

'Dressing.'

Yesterday, said the noon editions, there were seven thousand contacts traced and vaccinated. The number of total applicants

31

for vaccination was expected to rise to ten thousand by this evening. People seeing the queues outside the clinics were joining on. Stocks of vaccine were heavily drawn upon, but deliveries from London were reaching the town within ninety minutes of a telephone-call. There was no likelihood of a sudden scarcity.

'. . . Until Friday. That's important.'

'Yes. Thank you.'

'How's our fainting case?'

'All right. He's going in a minute, Mrs. Monks.'

By tomorrow, twenty thousand. We haven't started, yet.

Yellow and crimson, mingling.

'Will I feel bad, for a bit?'

'A little groggy, perhaps. You'll be able to work, though.'

'I've got to. I drive a bus.'

His big back blotted out the light from the doorway as he went away, hitching his coat on.

'I'm ever so sorry, Miss. I don't know what happened.'

His glasses glinted up at her. His face was white and old and bewildered.

'You felt rather odd, that's all. Better now?'

'Yes. Yes, thank you. I wanted to say how sorry I am.'

'You were very good. Don't take the dressing off till Friday, and don't scratch at it.'

'No. Thank you. I'm ever so sorry.'

'A lot of people do it. Have a good night's sleep.'

'Yes.'

He went away, his shoulders ashamed.

'Right up, please. And hold steady.'

Ten thousand, twenty thousand, thirty. A matter of noughts. Yellow and crimson and noughts, and wet umbrellas.

'Sleeve up.'

Their feet shuffled.

The rain stopped before midnight and left the streets bright under the lamps. The last bus had gone, to anywhere. Outside the two vaccination-clinics, paper was scattered: sweet-bags, cigarette-packets. The worried minds, soothed by glucose and nicotine, had been taken home and given a pillow; but windows were still lit; the night refused to pass.

'Everything seems worse at night, dear, when you can't sleep.'

'I know. I know.' The pillow was hot. Women were so dreadfully logical. 'But I've had this sore throat two days, now.'

'It'll go, dear. We all get sore throats.' Men were such dreadful babies.

A light in a window went out; another came on. A taxi prowled through Rutland Square, its tyres hissing along the wet roadway.

32

Steven Monks dropped Collins off at the Town Hall and came on home, stopping the car outside the house. He would leave it there. Sidelights? Strictly, but. . . . He turned them off. A sheen of light from the street-lamp struck obliquely across the wind-screen, and he gazed at the strange mottling on the glass, trying to think what it was. They looked like finger-prints. He rubbed one of them out, his left arm heavy. Julie's fingerprints. She had put her hands on the glass, touching it again and again to emphasise what she had been saying. . . . 'So it's been in the town nearly three weeks. . . . This isn't just an isolated case – it's the start of an outbreak.' And then: 'Oh darling, you're such a damn' fool, sometimes. You know we can't leave, now. . . .'

He rubbed the marks off the windscreen. He shouldn't feel this resentment. There was too much to do, and it had no real basis.

He got out of the car. Everything always had a real basis. He was lying to himself because he was dog-tired at the end of a fifteen-hour day.

Was she home?

The pavement smelled clean, and glistened under the street-lamp. Behind him the town was quiet. His ears buzzed with its silence.

'Steven?'

She was in the study at the back of the house. There was a tray of cheese and biscuits, and milk. 'Will this be all right, darling?'

She looked cool, calm, composed, at ease in her blue dressing-gown. But her eyes were tired; the lights hurt them. He switched one of them off and the room was changed, its shadows different.

He ate some cheese. Yes, he was tired. Yes, there was one new case. How was her day?

'Routine, mostly.' She nibbled biscuits with her small white teeth, competently, dropping no crumbs.

The milk was ice-cold from the fridge; he drank it slowly.

'The boys rang,' she said.

'Boys?'

She gave a tired smile. 'Ours.'

'Bill and Martin? What for?'

'They'd read about the Kingsbourne outbreak, and wanted to know if we were all right.'

He found an apple from the bowl. 'And were we?'

'I told them their father had the entire situation under control.'

'Whereas in fact their father had tried to make a bolt for it, but was brought smartly back on duty by the Nightingale.'

The crunching of the apple was loud in his head and the silence of the room. He should not have said that. The name for her was never used in fun. She had planned her life as a nurse, more than eleven years ago, a devoted, dedicated life; and had met Steven; and become merely a wife. He had told her once that it was quite plain she bore him a deep subconscious grudge that surfaced every so often. She had said, 'Possibly', and had tried to stop showing. Now it was driven deeper.

She had not answered. He said: 'It was nice of them to phone. Was there any other news?'

She had got up, to clear the tray away. 'I don't think so.' Her voice was light and sweet. Both the boys had that same *timbre*, for their voices wouldn't break for some years yet. Sometimes when they were home in the holidays he mistook their voices in the house. But her tone was now deliberate. She was turning the other cheek. And the other face came flashing into his mind – Ruth's face and voice and laugh. He got up suddenly as if she had really come into the room and he must ask her to go because Julie was here.

'More milk?' she asked, framed in the doorway.

'No, thank you.' He knew he must say something more, either to justify the sneer or change the subject. Anything, quickly, to stop the silence. 'Clifford's upset, about Ruth.'

Really in the room now, and named. Introduced by Clifford's disquiet.

'Oh?'

She stood in the doorway, the tray in her hands, the slim blue dressing-gown flaring out to the floor.

'She's keeping away from the town until this is over. I suppose he feels she ought to be here, to help him.'

There were no cigarettes on the mantelpiece.

'There are some here on the tray,' she said.

'I didn't see them.'

'I thought you'd want one, before bed.'

He took the packet and opened it. 'That was typically thoughtful of you.'

Her light grey eyes were red-rimmed. He must try to feel sorry for her. She took the tray out to the kitchen, saying over her shoulder, 'Poor Clifford.'

He followed her, lighting the cigarette.

'It's not like Ruth,' he said.

'Isn't it?'

'I mean, not to come and face it.'

'It isn't that, with Ruth. It would strike her as rather dreary.'

He could hear Ruth saying it. . . . Rather dreary. It was a pet expression, her most damning one. Julie had an ear for people's expressions.

'It won't help them,' he said.

'They're beyond help, surely.' Her movements were deft, rinsing the things and putting them to drain. He suddenly wanted to ask her: 'Have you ever dropped anything in your life?'

His cigarette was bitter. He had smoked too many today, had

seen too many frightened, selfish faces. He had spent fifteen hours in the atmosphere of the fear of death and his body and soul were soured with it.

He stared past her silhouette at the window, at the diffused glow of the street-lamp beyond, where the town was silent and sleep hard to come by.

'Clifford's too busy to worry much,' he said. 'He's got too much to do.'

'Or he sees to it that he has.'

'Do you think she should have come home?'

Julie turned and leaned her back against the draining board, the washing-up finished.

'I'm too tired, honestly, to talk about it. But if it's important to you, we will.'

'Of course not.' He looked away from her, to the glow of lamplight on the window. The window was frosted, with a pattern of round blobs, like her fingerprints on the windscreen. 'Did you give the boys my love?'

'Of course. They were very proud of you.'

Suddenly he swung away from her and almost shouted: 'What did you tell them *that* for? That I had the situation under control?' Looking back he saw she was shocked. 'Are you just rubbing it in, or what?'

She watched him without moving. He knew that look. She was pitying him. The silence held them both in close confinement. Neither looked away from the other.

'We're dead-beat, Steven.'

He flicked his half-finished cigarette into the sink-basket.

'All right, we're dead-beat. But I don't understand this plesaure you take in rubbing my nose in the dirt. I'd done a lot of hard work and I felt like a holiday. I'm not the only doctor in this town! We went on leave even when there was a war on, didn't we?'

The light hurt his eyes and the taste of the cigarette was foul in his mouth. Her look was so strange that he realised there had once been a time when they had never seen each other; and, oddly, this helped him. He could see her as a person, a stranger, dissociated from all the memories that condition the relationship of two married people.

Strangers could be courteous, accepting or rejecting each other's ideas, without the fear of future recrimination. There wasn't a future for strangers. He said more quietly: 'I just don't feel ashamed of wanting a holiday, and I don't want you to try making me ashamed. You can't, Julie.'

She looked down. 'It's not often we have a bust-up, is it?'

'This isn't a bust-up.'

'For you, it is. You're awfully worried about this, and if I could

35

only think what's it's really about, I'd try to help.' She folded her arms and moved away from the draining-board, towards the door. 'I'll tell you what, old boy. We're both so damned tired that we can't think straight.' When he turned round she was in the doorway, looking back at him. 'Do you think we could call it a day, and talk about it tomorrow, if you still want to?'

'There's nothing to talk about. We'll call it a day, for good.'

She left him standing in the kitchen, with the glow of the boiler on the tiled floor, and the drip of a tap at the sink. Now she had gone, he could relax, and not care what expression was on his face. But it was just as hard, alone here with the silence and the bleak late glare of the light, to think with honesty. A lie leapt up to protect him the moment there was a risk of exposing himself to himself, or Julie to injustice, or the risk of going too deep and finding something – admitting something – that could wreck them both. Eleven years was a long time, and it was too late to think of failure.

He should have gone away without her. She had been right to suggest it. But there was the risk there, too, and he had seen it coming. The idea of leaving her in Kingsbourne was followed in that instant by another: of ringing up Ruth.

It had been unthinkable, and so he had come back. But this couldn't go on. There had been too much of Ruth in his life. He was beginning to hate her.

'Steven?'

He froze at the sound of Julie's voice on the stairs. It was as if she had thrown open the door and found him doing something unforgivable.

'Yes?'

He went to the hall, and looked up at her.

'You didn't leave any sidelights on. I thought you should know.'

'It doesn't matter.'

Her fair hair hung down at one side as she stood halfway up the stairs, her face turned to him and catching the light from the street through the glass above the door.

'You look pretty,' he said.

'I don't feel pretty, Steven.'

He could hear the note of fright in her voice, and was astonished because he had never heard it before. It bewildered him. She had dropped something, and was too scared to look to see if it was broken.

'We're all right, Julie.' His voice sounded hollow in the long bare hall as he stood looking up at her.

FOUR

Rooks were building in the elms of Market Square, and the staff of the Health Department heard them cawing, but had no time to look out of the windows. They were busy with their lists.

There were now seventeen urns in Kingsbourne Crematorium. They contained the ashes of Charles Prebble, railway-clerk; Dolly Williams, usherette; Ralph Hodgson, stockbroker – and others: Joseph Moss, Mary Hewlett, Frank James Burton – and others: a bus-conductor, a prostitute, a wing-commander's wife. The urns were all the same shape.

Three of these people had been Catholics, but special dispensation had been obtained from their Church and their bodies had been burned in the cleansing fire for the sake of the living.

Four days ago the first cortège had moved up the driveway below the cedar trees. Immaculate cellulose was dulled by the drizzle, but the chromium and the glass were bright, and there was the glow of flowers. It had the air of a funeral, although the essentials were absent. There were no undertakers here, and no mourners, and the hearse was an ambulance.

The first of them, Charles Prebble, had lain in the iron cot for two hours longer, while it was decided how to rid the world of his remains. Dr. Preston had telephoned the superintendent of the hospital:

'I'd like to move him as soon as I can.'

'There's a snag, I'm afraid. The undertakers refuse to handle these dead.'

Preston had stared out of the window, gazing at the rain through his ghostly reflection. 'Why?'

'Someone's told them they're liable to gross contamination. Of course it's true.'

The rain dripped from the eaves, splashing on to the window-sill. Preston was only half-attentive. The dead were not his concern.

'We'll have to move him out, sir. You'll have to do something quickly.'

'I'm not exactly sitting here picking my nose, Preston.'

'Good,' Preston had answered before ringing off.

Volunteers came forward within an hour. Men of the ambulance service would act as pall-bearers, and the disinfection and rodent-control staffs of the Health Department would handle the corpse. Protective clothing was issued.

They followed Charles Prebble up the gracious drive of cedar trees, and dressed up like space-men in a small cold room of the chapel. The holy man intoned.

The wife of the deceased had been told: 'There'll be a full funeral service, you see. A full, proper service. The ashes will be placed in an urn, so that when you and your family can leave the house we can arrange for a memorial service, and you can tell us whether you'd like the ashes scattered, buried, or walled-up in a casket. There won't be much difference from an ordinary funeral, will there?'

'No. People are going to such a lot of trouble.'

'The circumstances are difficult, Mrs. Prebble, but that's no reason to withhold our respects to the departed.'

She turned suddenly and said, 'Get back in there!' One of the boys had opened the door an inch, and was listening. She didn't mind the boys listening, if they must; but Daphne was in there with them, and it would make her worse to hear these things.

The clock ticked on the mantelpiece.

'You've been very helpful, Mrs. Prebble. We realise how you and your children are feeling, in your sudden bereavement. . . .'

'Yes. . . .'

'. . . Do all we can, of course, to ensure . . .'

'. . . I see . . .'

'. . . And the will of God.'

He looked at his watch.

'You can come out,' she said, when he had gone.

Sid had said: 'That bloke can spout all right.'

He was told not to be wicked.

The screen of the television-set was flickering and they tuned the knobs. Mrs. Prebble sat down, seeming to do it without moving, to be composed, suddenly, in the chair, her hands on her lap, her eyes on the flickering screen. It was a godsend, that thing. They had wanted to take it away, because of the payments; but someone had paid them, and the set was still here. Their eyes were red with looking at it and their heads ached every night on the pillow; but they couldn't have managed without it.

'Is it ours now, Mum?'

'I don't know, dear.'

In an urn.

'We'll 'ave to take care of it now, then, Sid, if it belongs to us.'

She had seen one, in a museum. It was only small. Could they ever get Charlie in there?

'Where you goin', Mum?' They looked concerned.

'Nowhere.' She pulled at the door and left them silent and frightened in the small front room, and then they heard her being sick in the yard at the back.

38

The holy man intoned, and the others stood in their protective clothing, their mica visors already steaming-up.

'*We meekly beseech thee, O Father, to raise us from the death of sin unto the life of righteousness. . . .*'

Through the steam of the visors, the group appeared to be standing in some primeval place, isolated from the clarity of the realistic world.

It was hot, in here.

They shouldn't be here at all. The undertakers ought to be doing this lot. There was enough to do, with this show on, without standing about here. Call themselves undertakers? A lot of black velvet and purple, and respectful notices and Rolls-Royces done up to the nines, till it came to the push. No, thank you, mate. It's inconvenient, just now.

'*The grace of our Lord Jesus Christ, and the love of God. . . .*'

They say there's another one. A girl. One of the girls up at the Royalty. Poor little bitch. She won't be the last of them, either, this rate. Just think, if we'd known Jack Hawkins was there that week, we'd've gone there, instead of down the Palais. You can't never tell, these days, what's going to get you next. If you get across the road safe, there's a bloody jet coming down on your house if you don't die of cancer through smoking thirty a day – and that's peacetime, that is, without the bloody atom-bomb waiting to blow the lot up in one go.

I'll give them bloody inconvenient. This is their job.

It seems worse, somehow, with a girl. Only young, they said. A girl can be a mother, any time, so there's kids gone, too, when you look at it like that.

'*. . . and the fellowship of the Holy Ghost, be with us all ever-more.*'

That's it, mate, and about time too.

'*Amen.*'

Even under the protective clothing there was the reek of formalin. You never got used to it.

Off you go, Charlie, through the curtain and not a sound. If the rollers stick we'll come and give you a push. You're best out of it. At least you don't have to worry any more, like us.

The Chief Sanitary Inspector had a call from the M.O.H. in the late afternoon of Saturday, when the outbreak was entering its second week. In Mr. Buckridge's office sat Father MacGuire, watching him as he spoke to Tewson on the telephone.

'It's got to be done,' said Buckridge. 'All we have to tell them is that it's got to be done, and they've got to do it.'

'In theory,' came Tewson's voice.

'In practice. I've been told to cut red tape right out, and they'll have to do the same. This is a plague.' His voice was pitched too high. He must try to relax. More reasonably he asked: 'Has the Army made up its mind yet?'

'There's a disinfection unit arriving tonight, by road, with troops to handle it——'

'Where?'

'The playground behind St. Martin's. The area's being roped off now.' There was a pause. 'Can you attend a conference during the tea-break, Henry?'

'If I must. Who's coming?'

'A Ministry of Health liaison officer, and their infectious diseases expert, down from London.'

Impatiently Buckridge said: 'What do they know about smallpox that you don't?'

'They're here to help. There's always something to learn.'

Buckridge lowered his tone again. 'I'll be there, at five.'

When he had put the receiver back, Father MacGuire said: 'I'll go now.' MacGuire was an apple-faced man with black eyes and a shaven head. He would have looked better in Rome five hundred years ago.

'There's not much more to tell you, Father.' Buckridge had red eyes and a pallor. 'Gradually, the town is being cut off. Some trains have been taken off the schedule and others diverted. Nobody wants to come here, just now, and we've asked people not to leave unless it's urgent. The bus services to the country are cut. In the town three cinemas have closed, and both theatres. Two schools are closed – King's House and the County – and St. Martin's will stop work today because parents are keeping their children away – that's why we've been able to cordon off the playground at the back, for the Army unit.'

He saw another note on his pad.

'The box factory, too,' he said. He had an image of silent machines.

MacGuire got up, and stood looking down at his shoes, which were as black and bright as his eyes.

'In your opinion, when will the tide turn?'

'It's still coming in. We're visiting seven thousand contacts a day. There are twenty-five confirmed cases being nursed, and the death-roll is now seventeen. At present there's no case of smallpox that we can't link up with the known routes of infection – but that isn't to say there won't be, at any time. Ask me again in six days.'

'Six?'

'The incubation period varies, with this disease. The average is about twelve. Six days ago, an usherette at the Royalty Cinema was taken ill. She'd been working as usual, although there was the preliminary rash on her. She was at that time infectious. It was a popular film and a full house of thirteen hundred people.'

Father MacGuire watched him steadily. His mouth had contracted into a thin pinch.

'With the help of the Press and the emergency information bureaux, we've traced those thirteen hundred people, warned them of their risk, vaccinated them and put them on our observation list. But for the next six days they can only wait, and so can we.'

Someone came in, putting a file of papers on the desk.

'Master-list, sir.'

'Thank you.' Buckridge looked down at the twenty-two ruled columns. They swam before his eyes and when he looked up he saw the priest swaying. He pressed a call-button and said: 'I should like some more coffee, please.'

MacGuire said: 'Can't someone take over from you?'

'People do. There's my deputy and his assistant.'

'Then it's time one of them took over.'

Buckridge's smile splintered his face. 'They look worse than I do.'

'I wish I could do your job.'

'You could. Anyone could. It's clerk's work. But I couldn't do yours.'

Father MacGuire took the list of relatives from the edge of the desk, folded it and put it away. He said: 'You're one of those who could,' and went out of the office.

'There's a conference at five o'clock, Mr. Buckridge, in Dr. Tewson's office.'

Buckridge swung his head. A girl stood in the doorway. He had never seen her before.

'Who are you?'

'Extra staff, sir.'

The telephone rang and she went away while he was answering it.

'We've filled in the gap——'

'Who's that speaking?'

'Bennett, sir.'

'Where from?'

'A place called the Sombrero. It's an espresso bar behind the Post Office in Hillside. Jack Prebble was in here on the seventh, Friday. He was here about half an hour.'

Buckridge made notes. Jack Prebble was the carrier. It had taken a long time, this.

'That accounts for all his movements. He was there from ten-thirty to eleven that morning, was he?'

'As far as we can check, sir. But it fills the gap, all right.'

'I'll confirm it. Thank you, Bennett.'

He asked for an outside line and got through to the nursing-home where the boy was being looked after.

'There's an espresso coffee-bar called the Sombrero. Can you remember going there on the first Friday – the seventh?'

'Coffee-bar. . . .' The voice was thin and cold, hardly daring to speak.

'It's behind the Post Office, in a street called Hillside.'

The line was silent for seconds before the voice crept in again.

'What was it called, sir?'

'The Sombrero. An espresso bar.'

In a moment: 'I went into a place for a cup of coffee, that day. Has it got a big photo on the wall, sir? Photo of some French place? A seaside place, with white yachts. Not coloured, though.'

'If it has, that was the place where you had your coffee, was it, Jack?'

'Yes, sir. I remember it. I should have thought of it before.'

The boy would flay himself alive again, for forgetting.

Buckridge ended the phone-call as he had ended all the others. The boy wouldn't take any notice, but he must say it.

'We can't remember everything, Jack. You've helped us more than we'd hoped you would. It wasn't your fault. It's silly to go on thinking it was your fault. It could have happened to anyone.'

Putting the receiver down, he felt he was stamping out that thin haunted voice with his boot. For two days, they had told him at the nursing-home, all Jack had done was to sit and say – 'My dad's dead. My dad's dead. My dad's dead.' They had tried to stop him, but it was no use, so they left him alone to go on saying it, and thinking it, until he had begun shouting things and they had to dope him for the night.

He was much better now, they said. Not a nuisance any more. Just dead, himself, inside.

Buckridge reached for the telephone and stopped thinking about Jack. No one could help him now, but there were other people who needed help. He told the girl at the switchboard: 'Ring up the Sombrero coffee-bar, in Hillside. Ask them if they've got a blown-up photograph of a continental seaside resort on the wall – in black and white, showing white yachts.'

He made her repeat the details before he rang off. She was three minutes.

'It's a picture of Cannes,' she said. 'There's white yachts, too.'

He thanked her and buzzed his admin.-clerk.

'There's a new focus of infection,' he said. He looked at his hand lying on the desk as he told the clerk about the espresso café. The skin of his hand was white and the veins blue. You would be looking at your hand, like this, or your face in the mirror, or your wrists – especially your wrists and round the groin – and you would suddenly see a spot, and another, and you'd realise you had a rash.

'In Hillside. Yes. Friday the seventh. He was there roughly

42

between ten-thirty and eleven in the morning.'

And the pain in the small of your back would be significant, now. It connected: the pain, the rash. And so this was you, and this was your rash and the death you were going to die, just when you weren't ready for it.

'Bennett is tracing contacts from there. I'll get him to ring you direct, and you can add them to the duplicate lists.'

You were never ready for it.

'I'll let you know, after the conference in half an hour.'

As he put the switch down the telephone rang and he answered it.

'Bennett here again, sir.'

'Where from?'

'A flat in Oakwood Close. Number 33, Oakwood Close. Name of Whitcomb.'

Mr. Buckridge noted the details on his pad, because Bennett was speaking slowly and clearly. 'Yes?'

'It's Miss Betty Whitcomb. She's a waitress at the Sombrero. When we got here we found she was ill in bed.'

The name was down on the pad. Betty Whitcomb. She was now officially a member of the nightmare.

'Degree of contact?'

'Probably first, sir. She was serving at the tables, that morning. I've seen the roster.'

'Vaccinated?'

'No.'

Figures clicked through Buckridge's head. Her chances went down from 95 per cent to 30. He said:

'Have you got a doctor there?'

'No.'

'I'll send one. Report contacts as you find them. We'll keep Extension 26 clear for you.'

'Yes, sir.'

Buckridge clicked the contact and asked the switchboard for the M.O.'s office. Tewson was there. He never left it, now.

'There's a new spot,' said Buckridge. 'A café.'

Tewson said: 'A café. That's nice.' He wrote down the details as Buckridge gave them to him. A house was worse than a cottage. A block of flats was worse than a house. A café was worse than a block of flats. A hotel was worse than a café, unless of course there were cracked cups at the café. At most cafés, there were.

'Hillside.'

'The girl's home is Number 33, Oakwood Close. Will you send one of your team there?'

'I will, Henry.'

When they had rung off, Buckridge got up and took a red

paper flag from the drawer of the desk, and stuck the pin into the map at the spot where the Sombrero would be.

There were fourteen red flags on the map now. It looked like a field in Flanders.

The room at the back of the house was quiet. The drizzle that had now been settled over the town for twenty-four hours was collecting in gutters, puddling in backyards and along the pavements. It sent heavy drips falling from the eaves on to the glass roof of the conservatory, and Julie was consciously aware of the sound.

Rain was an imprisoning weather, closing in upon houses and the people in them. The world was smaller, brooding with a shut face against windows, and children couldn't go out. The mind was turned in on itself, its thoughts more secret and enclosed.

Julie listened to the drops falling, their sound reminding her of loneliness. Then she began writing neatly and competently, though her tired body sat slack in the upright chair.

Dear Monkey . . .

A fond name, not like his name, sometimes, for her – 'the Nightingale'.

They're appealing again for volunteers, up at the hospital. I decided not to go, the first time, because I thought I could be useful to you here in the house. Then I compromised, when I saw there was nothing much to do, and helped them out at the vaccination clinic. But anyone can scratch arms, and they're not short of people. Now I'm going to the hospital. Please don't be——

She turned her head to look at the bright wet sheen on the glass roof through the doorway. Please don't be what? Angry? He was angry now, about something. Or very troubled, with only the anger showing, as a defence.

'Why did you tell them *that*?'

She had told them that, because they were proud that their father was a doctor. That's all, Steven. It was said out of kindness. But it made you angry. Angry with yourself, for wanting to go off on a holiday, with an outbreak starting? Probably. It wasn't a good thing to do, and not like you. But there's something more than that. I don't know what it is, and I wish to God I could have asked you last night in the kitchen. But I might have made it worse. I'm too logical. Too competent. The Nightingale. You married a nurse. I wanted to marry you, and marry a doctor, but you only wanted to marry me, and not a nurse. But that's what I am. I'm sorry. Please don't be . . . worried.

– worried about me. I've been vaccinated, and can't catch it. And they do need people up there, badly. Not many volunteers for a job like that. Only Nightingales.

Oh, darling, do I really look as if I wear a stiff starched collar and a bun, always? What a horrible idea – you should divorce me, on grounds of competence. But I'm not competent right through. I like people, all people, and hate it when they're sick, and want to help them. I can't put that in writing, because it would look as if I considered myself a smug little paragon. Can people be one, without knowing it? Did you marry a smug paragon in a starched collar, with a bun? No wonder you hate me.

Not always, I know. Just last night, in the kitchen. The stove was glowing on the red tiles, wonderfully cosy; but it felt like standing in a bitter wind with you, and you had to shout above it. And even then I couldn't hear you properly – only the shout, not the meaning.

I wish I could help you. I hate it when people are sick, or troubled – you, of all people.

The writing on the paper looked unsteady.

She straightened her back, to stop the ache. There'd be a chance of sleep, at the hospital, with regular shifts and a roster.

It looked horribly smug, that last sentence. She turned the full-stop into a comma, and went on:

who think they're indispensable in a crisis. But all I can do is wash out bed-pans and take temperatures. That's what I've decided to do, for a few days. Mrs. Chalmers will look after you, and I've arranged everything about food, clean things, and the tradesmen. Don't tire yourself out, darling. See you soon.

Julie.

She put 'Mr. Steven Monks' on the envelope, in case Mrs. Chalmers came in first. For a long time she held it, wanting to open it and put a P.S. *The thing is that I'd rather be out of the house, when you don't like me very much. And so would you.*

He might not understand that she was saying it without any bitterness. People couldn't like each other all the time.

She put the note on top of the apples in the bowl, because she knew he would go there for one when he came home.

The main presses had stopped running soon after midnight and the place smelt of hot oil, paper and molten lead. Naked light-bulbs hung above the machines and along the walkways between them. Faces were pale. These men were the night-shift. They stood round Gracey, their editor, whose ruff of red hair was like a halo round the shiny white dome of his forehead.

To the men who worked here on the *Kingsbourne Gazette* the silence was unnatural after the clatter of the machines; but to the others it seemed merely a quiet place. Most places were quiet at one in the morning.

A man was rolling his sleeve down gingerly over the cross of adhesive tape, coming to the group who stood round Gracey. Dr.

Monks and the nurse worked on while Collins made his notes and his assistant moved among the typesetters and sub-editors and reporters. Their answers were subdued. They gave their names, their addresses, the names of their families, and pictured their families at home as they told their names to this official who was not to know that Emily Maud Barrett was really Em, with brown eyes and too much lipstick and a way of sniffing into her handkerchief and never blowing her nose properly. Emily Maud Barrett was a name for a monument or a cargo-steamer, yet it was really Em they wanted to know about.

'Yes, she got vaccinated two days ago. So did the children.'

'Which school do they go to, the children?'

'There's a boy and a girl. The boy goes to St. Martin's. The other one goes to the Secondary.'

He watched the pen moving. So Em hadn't been such a wet to go and panic them all down to the clinic, after all. They were safe now. He felt humiliated. He hadn't looked after his family by telling them to go and get vaccinated, the first day the news came in to this place. He'd called Em a wet, and told her she was panicking over nothing. She'd never let him hear the last of this.

'And your name, please?'

'Smith. Sub-editor. Thirty-two. Married.' He'd heard the order of the questioning, and saved them all time by trotting in out.

'Address?'

Somebody at the fringe of the group gave a sudden laugh and the others turned their heads. Old Piper. He'd laugh at his own funeral.

'What's going to happen, then?'

Gracey the editor said: 'God knows, Jim. If they clear the lot of us out of here we'll have to raise a skeleton crew from the other papers, I suppose.'

'What about pay?'

Lofty Ducker said: 'What do we care about pay so long as we don't break out in a rash?'

Their feet shuffled and no one answered. They didn't like the word. Rash was a rotten word and they'd seen too much of it here, where they got the news first and had to keep on printing it.

Steven applied the lymph. 'You feel perfectly fit?'

'Yes, Doc.'

The fierce cold lamps cast a shine on the bared skin.

'Are you a personal friend of this man Calcott?'

'No. We only work here.'

The skin came up in goose-pimples, sensitive to the irritant of the needle, right down the arm.

'Press that on tight, will you?'

Steven turned away, taking a swab from the nurse.

'Three more, Doctor,' she said.

46

He nodded. He knew she was frightened of him. His temper had risen very gradually through the day, and the climax had come in the evening. when he and Collins had started a bitter argument about whose duties lay where. They were both frazzled, but it had been Steven's provocation and he knew it.

'You feel perfectly fit?'

It was no good making the excuse that they were all dead on their feet, because the work had to be done, and there was no one else to do it. Even with reinforcements drawn from the outlying districts and London, they were doing a steady twelve to fourteen hours a day of monotonous routine work; but this was an emergency.

A plague, old Buckridge always said. 'This is a plague.' The phrase had lost its first dramatic effect, but he kept on using it when he was trying to impress someone. He seemed to *like* using it, as a man likes watching the snake that repels him.

'Are you a personal friend of this man Calcott?'

It was getting too tough for some of them. Today one of the inspectors had opened the front gate, walked up the path, knocked at the door, and lost his memory. When they opened the door he just said: 'I don't know why I've come here.' Steven had reached the house a few minutes later to find him drinking tea, his mind a blank. He was apologising to the woman all the time, to cover his fright. Why had he called at this house, and who was he?

If one link breaks in a long chain of mental routine, the lot goes, for a time.

'Press it on tightly, will you?'

The face of the nurse was scared. The whole town was scared, of smallpox or loss of memory or a doctor's temper. Fear was everywhere, of everything, spreading as indiscriminately as a disease, eating into the morale of a hundred and fifty thousand people already undermined by emergency conditions and restrictions.

'Will it be sore?'

'Yes.'

In the early days there had been the time and the spirit to say, 'Oh, just a bit, but nothing to worry about. Try to forget it, that's the best thing.' Now the answers came directly; there was a certain pleasure in dismaying people who weren't strong enough to take an honest answer.

'The last one, Doctor.'

He looked round at them, his clothes sticking to him, his eyeballs stinging. 'The man with the red hair. He's not been done yet.'

'Mr. Collins says he's been vaccinated a little time ago, when he was——'

'Get him here and don't damn' well argue with me!'

Who did she think she was, the Nightingale?

One Nightingale was enough to have about the place, looking at him as if he's committed some unspeakable crime in just wanting a holiday. God, what a priggish, self-sacrificing gaggle of saints they were!

If she were there when he got home, he'd just have a glass of milk and turn in. And not say anything. If either of them said anything there'd be another bust-up, like last night.

Remember, say nothing. It was important. Remember.

'What's the situation, Doctor?'

The swab was cold. If there were a hell, it would be thick with the stink of ether.

'You feel perfectly fit?'

'Yes. Always am.'

Then try a dose of this cowpox, and see how you feel in two days' time.

'Are you a personal friend of this man Calcott?'

'I meet him sometimes at pubs. We have a drink.'

'You go to his house?'

'He's got a flat. No. Why?'

It might be amusing, just this once, to answer one of their stupid questions. Very punctiliously, talking as if to a child. It might break the boredom.

'Because Mr. Calcott is dying of disease, and it follows that those people who work here with him might have caught it from him. Those people who work here with him and meet him socially as well, especially in his own home, stand a bigger risk still. You understand all that?'

'I think so.' The pale blue eyes under the halo of red hair were looking steadily at him. Their expression seemed to be pitying.

'Now press that dressing on tightly, please.'

'Right.'

The nurse looked frightened again, facing him.

'That,' he said carefully, 'is the last one.'

'Yes, Doctor.'

'I ought to be loaded with the stuff. I was only done last year, when I had to take a trip to Malaya.'

'I congratulate you. You're well protected.'

Gracey rolled his shirt-sleeve down. 'I know you're fagged out, but I'd like to know the situation. As the editor, I'm responsible for all these chaps, apart from getting the paper out.'

The nurse handed him his jacket, and Steven said:

'The situation isn't in my hands. Ask Mr. Collins, the man who told you it wasn't necessary to be vaccinated again. He knows all the answers, you'll find.'

Now he could clear out of here. They'd be spraying the place with formalin soon, and there was one stink worse than ether, and that was the stink of formalin, and the sweat of armpits under the rolled-up shirt-sleeves, and tobacco on the breath.

The clock on the wall said half past one. The figures had no significance. It had ceased to matter what the time was, what the day was. Time and place had become a single focal point in which they all lived. The middle of a plague.

He shut his bag and picked it up. They were all yapping now, and words came up from the hum. Evacuation. Skeleton-crew. Day-shift.

We've got to get the paper out.

Why had they got to? Did they think it was important?

Monks.

His own name, one of the words.

He told the nurse: 'You can get off now.'

'Yes, Doctor. Good-night, Doctor.'

They were all milling about, talking about their damned paper. He could see Collins, laying the law down.

'. . . A cup of tea, Doc?'

'What? No. No, thanks. I'm going home.'

'Over there,' someone said.

He bumped his arm against one of the machines, going down the walkway. Outside, there'd be a lungful of air to be had.

'Dr Monks.'

That's me. The Monkey. 'Which way out?'

'That door, and down the stairs. Good-night.'

'Good-night.'

The light-bulbs went past above his head, picking at his eyes.

'Dr. Monks!'

There was a man behind him.

'Yes?'

He turned and leaned one shoulder against the wall at the top of the stairs. His elbow throbbed, where he had banged it on the machine.

'Mr. Buckridge said you'd be here, Doctor. There's a message from the hospital. They're keeping your wife there – it's been confirmed, I'm afraid.'

Horn-rimmed glasses, a Rotary lapel-badge, thinning hair. One of Buckridge's men.

'What's been confirmed?' he asked the man.

'She was taken ill soon after she got there this morning.'

The lamps glared against his eyes. The effort of thinking straight was crippling.

'I'm Monks,' he said. 'Is it *my* wife you're talking about?'

'You ought to ring up the hospital. I expect you'll want to. There's a phone-box at the bottom of the stairs.'

FIVE

'And comforts?'

'We are all right.'

They stood facing each other, matron and priest each recognising the strength of the other as if they belonged to a secret society.

'Books?'

'Plenty. The superintendent's had a hundred pounds put at his disposal from the Hospital Group's Amenities Fund. We got through nearly all of it in one day, so there's nothing material we lack.'

There was a faint nostalgic thrill in her voice: there had been a small sudden Christmas, in the middle of the nightmare. A whole hundred pounds. It had been a bean-feast, a shopping-spree. A covered van had arrived, loaded with cigarettes, sweets, books, games and a vast bouquet of artificial flowers. There had been a dance in the dining-hall, and Simpson had put on a show for them with her cinematograph. It was the evening when the young mother had died.

'You'll let me go through the wards, Matron?'

She was fascinated by the brightness, the blackness, of his eyes. Her father had had eyes like these, staring the world out, strong.

'Let you? They need you.'

He held the door open for her. 'It is very difficult?'

She turned her head to look back at him steadily as she went through the doorway. 'For some of us. It'll be nice to pop into the town again.'

'I can bring anything you ask for.'

'We've more use for you than as an errand-boy, Father.'

She took him to the isolation wards.

Julie lay shivering in her fever. They were right about death: it wasn't fearful. It was the fear of dying that held you pinned down and alone. Soon you would be out of all this, and you would go alone, be really alone for the first time in your life, desperate for the bodily-remembered comfort of the womb. But this was the way chosen. Alone.

She seemed to be standing outside already, listening to the laughter on the other side of the door that had shut behind her.

Only one or two had noticed she had gone, and Steven had simply turned his head, wondering, his face bitter, a drink still in his hand, the music loud. Her mother had said that Uncle Robert drank too much, and stopped saying it when they found him in the barn, with the smell of the rope and the scratching of the dog in the wired run, always scratching there because they said he had killed a sheep. They had made him sick to see if there were wool in his stomach. Death was always sudden, a margin between minutes; but dying was a gamble, a snuffing-out of years of waiting, of knowing it, of trying to escape; and the sordid look of the bedclothes, the spilt medicines, the visitors with their frightened jollity.

She had never seen anyone visit a hospital and not go away with a lighter step even if the worst had been learned. The conscience knew more escape-routes than the heart. The sun was out again, a round blob expanding and contracting against her eyes. She kept them closed. Poor Clifford.

People spoke, their soft voices feathering through the air. The pillow had become a hot stone and her head rocked on it, the sun expanding and contracting. Poor Uncle Robert, with the new rope he had gone specially into the village to buy, but nobody knew. There was a little dell by the paddock, deep in blue-green nettles all the summer, and that winter they had found the bottles where he had been throwing them, a bright splintered heap glinting through the dead nettle-stalks. He must have been very lonely, throwing them there for nobody to know.

'If you can,' they said.

'If I can,' she said, and rocked her head on the hot stone. 'Poor Clifford,' she said.

The sun went out and she tried to resist the hands, pushing her whole weight against them.

'Alone,' she said. 'Going alone like Uncle did.'

Without any memory of sitting up and opening her eyes she was drinking the water. Her face was being sponged and she nearly spilt the water.

'If you do,' she said.

They took the glass away.

'You should let me sleep. It's the first thing you learn.'

'Stop chattering, or Father MacGuire will go. He can't stand women who talk.'

They took the stone away and put pillows behind her. The sun was on the wall, a white round globe. 'What's the time?'

'It's time you stopped dithering.'

As if to a child. The same wish to put comfort into words. A sick person is a child, remember, easily frightened and, grateful for comfort.

'What did you dope me with?'

'Mrs. Monks, this is Father MacGuire.'

'I'm not a Catholic.'

'I'm not a woman,' said the big man, 'but I've come to talk to you, just the same.'

'You shouldn't wake a sick person.'

Matron said: 'What gives you the idea you were asleep? I've a message from Dr. Preston. Yours is alastrim.'

'It's too early to find out.' She gazed up at the matron.

'Do you know how long you've been here?'

'All night.'

'All four nights. It's alastrim.'

'I don't need false comfort, thank you.'

'You're a blinking nuisance, you know.'

'And so are you. It's wonderful to sit here and tell a full-blown matron that.'

Father MacGuire said: 'I'm getting to know your husband.'

'Where's she gone?'

'Who?'

'Matron.'

'Along there. Do you want her?'

'No. Only to apologise. You know what sort of a person she is, Father? Do I call you "Father" even if I'm not a Catholic?'

'You can call me a blinking nuisance if you like.'

Her vision was clearing. 'I've not seen you before.'

'I haven't been in the town very long.'

'What did you say about my husband?'

'I'm getting to know him. I've been trying to think what his wife was like.'

'I hope it doesn't come as a shock.'

He was sitting on the bed, his big white hands on his lap. 'That was an odd thing you said just now. You said: "Going alone, like Uncle did." Is it a secret?'

'He was a secret drinker. Nobody understood him.'

'You mean he didn't understand himself.'

'Nobody does.'

'A few people do. Can I get you anything?'

'Nothing decent.'

He leaned his big body forward in a query, perhaps not catching what she said. She added carefully: 'I can't very well ask a priest for a bed-pan.'

'It's part of my job, really.'

'What is your job?'

'Helping and teaching.'

'Well you can't teach me much about bed-pans. I'm a qualified nurse.'

'Where are they kept?'

'I don't want one. I said it out of devilment. I'm such a smug paragon that I thought a break would do me good. I'd like to shout awful things at Matron, but the trouble is that I wouldn't mean them. She runs this place like a battleship and I admire competent people.'

Her eyes had closed of themselves, and she lay against the pillows. Father MacGuire watched her, and saw how pale her face was, under the hideous purple rash.

She was young, he thought. It looked a worse defilement on a young woman's face. It gave her a great dignity, he thought. Here she was, a pretty young woman, suffering the disfigurement of the thing that would soon kill her; and she did not complain. She was still herself, and was absolute and unchanged. Great dignity, in someone so slight and young.

'Have you come to give the last sacraments?'

'How could I have? You're not of my faith.'

'To comfort me, then. I don't want comforting. It isn't alastrim. I know that. I'm a nurse.'

'What's alastrim?'

'Or did you just come?' She opened her eyes, trying to focus them, realising that half the things she said were not really being voiced but only murmured in her mind. 'I mean, did they send for you, or did you just come?'

'I just came.'

She let her eyes close. It was too great an effort to watch him all the time. 'Did you meet me some time? Some time ago?'

He leaned closer. He wasn't quite sure he understood.

'I mean some time before? Clifford's an awfully good person. Too good. He gets hurt, a lot. Ruth hurts him.'

She had a child's mouth. She looked like a child with measles. 'I'm not frightened. I want that understood.'

Father MacGuire got up from the bed and leaned over her. He felt humility, as he always did when he was with someone dying. Their destiny was so magnificent and so nearly accomplished that he felt awe of them. Was it too much to ask of a mere human, this immense necessity of ridding the soul of the body? But it was happening again before his eyes and he felt humility.

'I'll come back, child.'

Her mouth puckered over some words he did not catch, and he bent over and kissed her brow.

'Darling Steven,' she said clearly.

His lips were sensible of the raised papules of the rash. When he turned away he saw the matrom coming towards him, and waited for her.

There was an odd light in her eyes, but her voice was unmistakably harsh. 'That was a stupid thing to do, Father, for a man of your wisdom. I hope you don't repeat it. In here we are exposed to gross contamination, all of us, every minute. There's no need for dangerous heroics.'

MacGuire looked down at her and was reminded that, no matter what people believed, height gave no advantage.

'She tells me you've a nasty temper, Matron.'

His bright black eyes were amused and she resented it.

'All I ask is that you don't do such a foolish thing again while in my hospital.' She turned away from him quickly and spoke to the nurse on her way out. Father MacGuire looked back once to the young woman in the bed. Certainly it had been a foolish thing to do, to give his kiss from pity and not for blessing.

The car had driven right up the West Road to the main building instead of halting at the gates like the ambulances and delivery vans. It was parked in the big forecourt, with the bag in the back, the ignition keys still swinging from the dashboard, her finger-marks still mottling the glass of the windscreen in the glow of the porch lamps.

Preston was in the dining-hall, beginning some cheese and biscuits and a glass of wine. Steven said:

'You live well, here.'

Preston looked up at him and motioned him to sit down at the end of the long bench. 'Hello, Steven. Will you join me? We blued a lot of money from the Fund – try a glass.'

Steven sat down, leaning against the wall, giving Clifford room to eat.

'I'd better not.' He was primed with Dexedrine, a heavier dose than yesterday. 'I've got more work to do.' He watched Clifford break a biscuit neatly in half and butter it. The sound of the knife on the plate sent an echo shivering along the deserted hall. Somewhere in the distance of the building they were washing-up.

'She's got alastrim,' Clifford said, and cut a wedge of cheese.

Steven sat with his body taut, hands rigid in his pockets, his legs crossed and throbbing.

'You wouldn't lie, would you?'

'No. It's alastrim. Congratulations.' He sagged over the edge of the table, but his face didn't look sleepless. They ran a schedule, here.

'A full test?' There should be a swamp of relief flowing and easing his body. He merely distrusted Preston.

'Yes.'

For a long time afterwards Steven always had the same thought whenever he put cheese on a biscuit or watched anyone else do it: So Julie is going to live.

Clifford said: 'We've had two or three others, highly modified. How did Julie pick it up, d'you know?'

The wall was chill against Steven's back and he kept his shoulders pressed against it, slaking the heat of his body. At some time during the day the sun had tried to shine, and the streets had been clammy with heat-mist, worse than the drizzle.

'At a café. The carrier had been there for half an hour. It's given us thirty-odd new contacts. I saw her name on the list before I came up here on Saturday night.'

The note-paper had smelt of apples, when he was reading it. It was as if she had already known and had come up here to die without waiting to be fetched.

'Her vacc. hadn't taken, of course. Why wasn't she checked?'

'Is Julie the sort?'

'Anyway, you're lucky.' He drank some wine, leaving a touch of cheese on the rim of the glass.

'Is that Brie?'

'Yes.'

'I think I'll have some.'

Clifford nudged the plate along. 'You always were a well-disciplined type. Why don't you break down sometimes? Men don't cry enough, these days. It was better when they did. Now they die early of heart-strain.'

Steven took some biscuits. 'I suppose I don't believe it, yet.'

'It's given you an appetite, that's something. Help yourself from the bottle – sorry we've only got tumblers.'

Drinking the wine, Steven tried to realise what had happened. He had believed he was in the middle of a nightmare, dragging his big personal fear along through the business of the crisis – the fear that he had lost touch with his stars, had lost his direction and his place. Then there had come the real nightmare, with the little man's horn-rims flashing in the glare of the lights, the Rotary lapel-badge giving him identity as he stood there worried with news. The thought, then, at the top of the stairs with the smell of oil and paper and molten lead, had been: So Julie is going to die.

Now it was over. He could forget all the images that had flickered through the night in the name of sleep: himself in the house alone without Julie – without her *anywhere*, not just absent from him. And Ruth, haunting him until he woke hating her, until the revulsion ran its course and he was obsessed again with the thought of Ruth in this new terrible situation, Julie gone.

He had tried to make her understand, when he had come up here that night. It should have been easier, because there hadn't been time to think. If she was going to die, she had to know about this thing that was happening to him: this appalling loss of direction symbolised by his determination to get away from the town at the moment when they would all be needed here urgently to fight the outbreak. His odd resentment had bewildered him until he faced the possibility that he had wanted to take Ruth away with him instead of Julie, and mustn't. Then the chance of

55

going away even with Julie looked like being jeopardised by the diagnosis of smallpox; and the resentment had increased so that he had become desperate to leave the hospital and the town.

There had been something of panic in him that morning, and this frightened him. Panic was a suspense of reason. But he was a disciple of reason. Clifford knew that. 'You always were a well-disciplined type.'

He had lost his way. For twenty years he had been first a doctor, then a man. Now this woman Ruth had found the man in him and he came first.

Julie had said, that night: 'I've been infectious and contagious for the last two days, darling. I want you to have a test.'

'Don't keep worrying about me . . about *me* . . .'

Her face was pale, her eyes large, and he had looked at her knowing the bug was in her, beginning slowly to kill her; and he could not listen to her worrying about him. The last of his self-respect had crashed down the stairs with a thunder that shivered him, though the man in the horn-rimmed glasses never heard and never knew.

'I should have checked you for take,' he said to her. 'You hadn't taken.'

She said nothing, thinking of something different and then realising what he had said. 'It was my job, Steven. I was at the clinic the whole time. I just forgot. Steven – ' she looked up at him and right into him – 'if I die, will the boys be all right? You love them, don't you?'

She mustn't.

'Yes. I love you and them.' It had to be true. Everything else was unimportant, and Ruth an impotent slut. He must re-establish his direction. 'I wanted to explain why I was foul-tempered, Julie. It's not simple, and I'm funking it.'

'Then don't worry, darling. Is it all right?'

'It's going to be. I've got to work it all out, when there's time and a bit of peace. It came on me when I wasn't watching – you know what I'm trying to say? – and then I was in it, up to the neck, and——'

'Poor Steven. I'm not much help.' Her face was so white. He looked away from it. 'Tell them not to worry. Peter will be all right, but Martin will want some help——'

'You won't die. Listen——'

'I might. It's about fifty-fifty. Thank God we both know exactly what we're up against. Did you find my silly note?'

'Yes.'

'A fat lot of use I am, up here.'

He would never call her the Nightingale again. There had to be these unimportant comforting vows, made solemnly in the face of the knowledge that he might never call her by any name again.

'We are all right,' he said, and took her hand again.

'You mustn't touch me, Steven.'

'I touch what I like, and what I love.'

'That's beautiful, but you mustn't.' There was no strength in her to push his hand away, though she tried; and that was the moment when he couldn't stand it any more, and he had come away.

Clifford was right. Men didn't cry enough, these days. For the sake of decency they were expected to bottle everything up, outraging their biological mechanism.

'Did you tell the boys about this?'

He looked at Clifford. 'What was that?'

'Did you tell your boys about Julie?'

'No. There was no point.'

'A good thing, then.' Suddenly he was saying: 'I wish Ruth would have a child.'

Steven looked at him, seeing only one side of his face. His eyes were down, reflective. He had said it before, but not with this intensity.

Steven said: 'It wouldn't be difficult.'

'What?' He turned his head, taking his glasses off, so that Steven knew he was suddenly on the defensive. It was a movement that played for time. 'I wouldn't want to do it that way, by accident on purpose.' He polished the glasses: it would be absurd to take them off for nothing and people would guess.

'You're not a deceitful man,' Steven agreed.

'Apart from that, she must want one too. You can't expose a child to a one-sided parentage from birth. It'd be criminal.' He put his glasses on and for a moment stared at Steven with his pale eyes. 'We've not talked like this before, have we? Not in how many years? A good dozen, I suppose. Now you've just heard your wife isn't going to die, and I'm terrified I'm going to lose mine in a different way, and here we are sitting on a bench eating cheese and biscuits.'

He drained his glass of wine with quick defiance and for the first time Steven thought kindly of him, the first time in a good dozen years. So Clifford wasn't just a hard worker and a cuckold.

'It's time you asked people for help, you know.'

'I always find it difficult,' Clifford said. 'They've got enough worries of their own, especially at a time like this – but you –' he shrugged his hands.

'I've just had my reprieve.'

'Yes. You've a flair for phrasing things, haven't you. . . .'

Steven leaned forward with his elbows on the table, flexing the ache in his shoulders and spine. 'Clifford, you're not lying, about

57

Julie. You said you weren't. It's highly modified. But tell me again.'

A clatter came from the doorway at the end of the dining-hall as someone wheeled a trolley in, loaded with dishes. The echoes ran round them and filled the place. Preston pitched his voice rather higher. 'You can go and see the report for yourself. You'll have to believe that.'

More lights were being switched on. They realised they had been sitting in partial gloom. Clifford pushed his plate away and looked at the wine-bottle to see how much there was left, but didn't take any more.

She could be in the house again, writing her competent notes at the desk, turning her head to look up when he came into the room. What had she ever done to make him less than glad to see her, before? What had she done now, to make him yearn to see her there again? Nearly died. It was no reason; she hadn't changed. There must be another reason for this feeling.

'Does she know?'

'We've told her, of course. I don't think she believes it.'

The domestic worker who had wheeled the trolley in was singing, and Preston looked at her down the length of the hall. She was a fat woman with a cast in her eye, one of the volunteers from the Institution; she was singing something from an American musical He had been going through the main hall a week ago when she had come in, soaked from the rain. 'I've come to help,' she had said. 'Where do I go?'

The message that Ruth had left for him was brief: *I might as well keep out if the town's bug-ridden, mightn't I? Phone me if you want anything.*

'Let's get out of here,' Steven said, and got up stiffly.

The woman's voice called up the length of the dining-hall.

'Have you finished?'

Preston turned as he got up. 'Yes, thank you. I'm sorry we were late.'

'Time don't matter to me, nor never has.' She began singing again as they went out through the swing doors. In the passage Steven said:

'You don't really mean you're terrified about losing Ruth, do you?'

Preston walked slowly with his white jacket open and his hands in the pockets. 'Did I say that?'

Steven waited a moment and then asked him: 'Is she still in London?'

'Yes.'

'There's nothing she could do down here, is there?'

'No.'

He had closed up. Alone with Steven in the odd intimacy of

that vast deserted dining-hall he had been moved to confide; now he remembered himself. Walking beside him Steven was sorry for him. For the first time he felt pity for Clifford Preston: the indifference of a dozen years was going down. It was right – Julie hadn't changed, and there was another reason for these feelings. The change was in himself and it was unnerving. Was it apparent? Did Clifford detect it?

It would be strange to have to learn as late as this to be a friend of his.

'It doesn't concern me very deeply, Steven, but I'd like to get it straight.' He had stopped and was facing Steven in the corridor, pulling his glasses off and wiping them, his pale eyelids flickering with nerves as he looked down at them and with an effort kept his voice steady, saying: 'Have you and Ruth ever stayed anywhere together?' He looked up suddenly and faced him short-sightedly, the spectacles still in his hand. 'No, I mustn't leave any doubt as to what I mean. Have you ever made love to her?' The lights strained his eyes but he didn't put his glasses on yet, nor did he look away. The effort he was making thickened his voice. 'We're civilised people. There won't be a brawl. It's just that I want to know.'

The hot disinfectant water stung his skin, streaming over him from the shower. Someone was using the next cubicle; perhaps one of the ambulance men.

He was thinking of Sister Gill. She had said:

'I'd rather you didn't disturb her, Doctor.'

'Is she asleep?'

'Yes. She hasn't had much real sleep today.'

'Has the fever abated?'

'For the moment.' She didn't move from the doorway. Had he insisted, she would have allowed him to pass. 'You've been told it's not semi-confluent?'

'Yes.' Clifford had told him, sitting with his cheese and biscuits and the terror of losing his wife. 'In a different way,' he had said.

'You must be very relieved, Doctor Monks.'

'Yes. But one can't quite . . .'

'I know.'

She had soft eyes. He had asked the matron, once, how Sister Gill had earned her G.M., but nobody knew in detail. In the shelters under the Edgeware Hospital, they believed. He said:

'Then I won't disturb her.'

She moved a little from the doorway. 'She's been a wonderful patient, as you can imagine.'

'Thank you, Sister Gill.'

She turned away as a nurse came along the passage, hurrying and quiet. He thought: When a patient dies in a hospital, nothing is changed in people's faces; you would never know; yet you are immediately certain.

'Can I lend a hand, Sister?'

'Oh no, thank you. Dr. Maysfield's about.' When she had gone away with the nurse, he had stood for a moment longer outside the door. No sound came from the small room. She was sleeping. He could picture her face, as he had seen it so many times, side-ways on the rumpled pillow with the first light touching the window, the air stale in the room, a milkman clattering in the Square. Sometimes she played a game with him, lying with her eyes closed and breathing regularly and deeply for a time, then saying clearly: 'I'm awake.' Her eyes would open and she would smile. But how had she known he was watching her? It was not always with kindness, nor yet cruelty; but with a critical detachment. The world was never more clear than at first light.

He turned away from her door. They had not let him see her. The feeling of loneliness, suddenly upon him, still lingered as he stood now under the shower in the disinfection room, spinning the taps off.

The other man was paddling about in search of a towel, a big man with a pear-shaped body and fat buttocks. Steven said: 'On the rail.'

'What? Oh yes.' He turned round. 'It's Dr. Monks, isn't it?'

'Yes. You're Father MacGuire.'

They rubbed with their towels in the steam, their flesh anæmic-looking in the cold lights even after the heat of the water.

'I've just been talking to your wife. She was kind enough to receive me.'

'It was kind of you to visit her. You must have done her good; she's asleep now.' He pressed the towel to his face, imprisoning himself in its darkness and silence, relaxing his muscles, eased by its rough enveloping comfort. The priest's voice came from the distant outside world.

'I admire her so much.'

The light burst in as he took the towel away and began stropping. 'My wife?'

'Yes. She'd no time for me, but still did her best to entertain me. My intention was to comfort her if I could, but the idea went out of my head as she talked to me.'

'That does sound a little like my wife.'

Father MacGuire raked at his ears with the towel, watching Steven as if sizing up his strength. 'How much is the danger?'

'Practically none.'

The priest stared at him, the black eyes glittering as the thoughts struggled for the answer. 'They were telling her she had alstrim. Was that it? Would it be? Alstrim?'

'Alastrim, yes.'

'What is that, please?'

'A mild form of smallpox, not dangerous.'

'She doesn't believe them. But it's true?'

'It's true, yes.'

MacGuire's big face looked suddenly smooth and his eyes sparkled. 'How you must feel. . . . How you must feel. . . .'

Steven dropped the towel on to the bench and found the clean dressing-gown that had been left for him. His movements were growing slack; the effective peak of the Dexedrine had passed. There was some more in the dashboard pocket of the car. 'I'm not sure how I feel, really.' He tied the cord and looked up into Father MacGuire's unbelieving face. 'I mean I don't want to sing, or anything. It's much more than that.'

'Of course.'

'You don't understand me. It's more than delight and relief. I feel different about other people.' He turned for a cigarette and remembered they would have been destroyed. The last time he had been in here an ambulance man had left him one from the clean side.

'You believed she might die, before you heard this.'

'Yes.'

'Then you are taking stock. It usually happens.'

'You think so?'

'People who have lost someone have often told me: "If they could come back, everything would be different." You imagined what it would be like, without your wife. You must have. You suffered the horrors of the *fait accompli*. You must have thought: "If I could have her back, everything would be different." Now she is back, and everything is.'

Steven leaned in the doorway and in a moment passed the priest the clean dressing-gown. 'Come in here. This is the frontier for the bugs.'

MacGuire passed through and turned to look at Steven, his bare feet padding on the tiles. 'I wish that almost everything I say didn't sound like a rabid over-simplification.'

'I suppose the truth has that ring to it.'

'Not a bit. It's a most devious affair, especially when committed to a limited vocabulary.' He gazed at Steven as if he were trying to read him and then asked: 'Isn't it bad for her to go on thinking she's in danger?'

'They can't do more than tell her, and she's feverish. It doesn't always mean anything, at that stage.'

'Yes, she was rambling a little, when she spoke to me. But she felt she was going to die.' Ruefully, he said: 'She convinced me of it, and I've lived a lot with the dying.'

The terrible idea came to Steven: Perhaps she is.

'It's modified,' he said curtly. 'I've seen the report.'

The priest looked surprised. 'Of course.'

Perhaps she was, and only she knew. 'Does a person have second sight on the death-bed?'

'Not of anything in this world.'

Steven made another instinctive movement for a cigarette, and was disturbed by this indication of slack mental coherence. Long hours, lack of sleep, cigarettes and the drug . . . and the shivering cold of the nightmare that was now over. . . .

'My God,' he said, 'I'd like to get drunk. Really drunk.'

Father MacGuire nodded.

'It would do you a lot of good.'

'You think so?'

'It would be good for people like you.'

62

'Like me? What am I like?'

'A steel spring. But the people who need to get drunk are the kind who never do. They won't let themselves. But it's not the only way to unwind. It's the cheapest.'

'Scotch isn't so cheap.'

'I mean the cheapest in effort.'

Steven looked at him in his dressing-gown. It was too small for him. He had the pathetic appearance of a needy monk.

'You're telling me to pray.'

'Telling's no good. You'll come to it, when you can't stand doing without it. On the other hand you might force yourself to do without it all your life. But it's an odd kind of self-discipline, I always think.'

'Stupid, you mean.'

'No. Admirable.'

A cigarette would taste glorious and the smoke would go curling upwards. It was an unlucky thing to be closeted with a priest while the clothes were drying. And the man was a hypocrite.

'You can't really mean admirable.'

The bare feet of the priest made a flapping noise on the tiled floor as he moved slowly parallel with the wall, pacing like a prisoner; and Steven had to look down at the feet, struck with the odd feeling that they might be webbed.

'Yes, admirable.' He stopped and turned and looked at Steven. 'Admirable as a self-imposed undertaking, as an exercise in self-sufficiency, as an expression of independence, and as a show of spiritual strength.'

Steven looked round for the bench and sat on it, cupping his face in his hands to shut out the light and the sight of MacGuire's ridiculous dressing-gown. Through his fingers he said, 'I don't feel in the least spiritually strong at the moment.' He sat as slack as a drunk, listening to his own voice. It sounded detached from him. His own head couldn't be capable of thought coherent as this: his head felt like a saturated swab. 'In fact I don't feel *anything*.'

He was staring up at the priest and his hands had fallen away of their own volition. Angrily he said – 'I don't *feel* enough in my life!' He had shouted like this in the kitchen at home. He didn't question this flare of anger; it wouldn't have to matter. He liked shouting. 'These things are happening to me all the time and I'm not *feeling* them! I didn't love my wife and then she nearly died – or I believed she might die – and now she's not going to – and the most I can feel is that other people seem different now – *she's* different, too. I don't love her now – nearly dying isn't a reason for loving – for *being* loved by anyone – but I want her back with me!' He was standing up. He couldn't

63

remember getting up from the long scrubbed wooden bench. MacGuire was closer to him, nothing showing in the bland black-eyed face – 'You're listening, aren't you?'

'I'm listening.'

'It's not *enough*!' His hands were moving about. 'Maybe I'm changed by these things, but it's not enough. I ought to *feel* things about them – I ought to be *moved*!'

The shout seemed not to have come from him and the words hadn't been thought of before they were spoken. He was rather frightened by this. Could he stop himself shouting? He might say anything – something horrible or secret.

He turned away from MacGuire and tried to steady himself. Logic ran on in his head, explaining and justifying: long hours too many cigarettes and too much Dexedrine, and the nightmare that was over. Or just beginning. He looked round at the other man and again the shout broke out before he knew it was coming – 'I don't *register* anything!'

The priest's face seemed to have shrunk; his whole body looked smaller, yet he hadn't moved back. And there was an echo in the unfurnished confines where they stood.

'It isn't that you don't. You daren't.'

The priest's mouth was moving. The smell of the disinfectant was appalling now. This place was a tomb, reeking of putrefaction.

'I daren't?' But it was hard to relate even a repetition.

'You're frightened of having a heart, in case people might see it, and shame you.'

'Do I look all right?' He was suddenly standing within a foot of the priest, jutting his head out. 'How do I look?'

'Angry and frightened.' The man's voice was as distant as his figure was small.

'Be damned!' He was against the bench and could feel its edge behind his legs – this was why MacGuire had shrunk again. The reasoning cooled him. 'I've been shouting. I'm sorry.'

'It did you good.'

'You think everything does people good – getting drunk, shouting, making love to another man's wife – would you say *that* did me good? Would you?'

A door opened and someone said: 'Are you all right in there?'

The priest moved quickly, a big shadow against the wall, the shine on his face catching the light. 'Perfectly, thank you.'

He stood facing the doorway between the contaminated and the clean side.

'Is there anything you want?' the distant voice asked.

'Our clothes would come in handy.'

'They're nearly dry.'

Steven heard the door being shut. He was crouched on the

bench again. He couldn't remember sitting down. The shadow moved against the wall and MacGuire's voice was closer.

'Shouting is good because it's an outlet. Women cry. If in deep grief, very loudly. We have to unburden all we can of the agony and make others share it, make them realise that we have it and need help. Shouting and wailing are the simplest form of communication. We can't stand the suffering alone any more. Some body has to share it, and we feel angry when they don't seem to want to, and frightened that they won't. But don't worry. I can take all that you can give.'

It was bitterly cold in here now. This was a midnight place, the deciding-ground where all the world hung in the balance of one day's death and the beginning of another. Just because it had always happened it needn't happen now.

'You talk like a psychologist, not a priest.'

He could hear that his voice sounded calmer; he had not shouted. Perhaps it was over, then.

'Isn't a psychologist a scientist of the soul?'

'The meaning's changed, these days.' He didn't feel like arguing the point. He just wanted to be left alone. 'They're a hell of a time with our clothes. I'll see if I can agitate someone.' He got up from the bench, his muscles on fire again with the sudden movement.

Outside, the night was fresh. At the open doorway he stood and looked up at the frail web of cloud that was drifting below the stars, tearing itself here and there on their bright points and leaving gaps. Some of the peace of the night-sky came on him, and helped.

'Has the rain stopped?' The priest was behind him and Steven was aware of how close he was, of his size.

'Yes. It stopped a long time ago, you know. Before dark.'

'I didn't notice.' The cool air moved in against their faces. 'Do you remember everything you have just said to me?'

Someone was banging from outside, near the coke-dump, and Steven gave him a call, asking him to hustle up their clothes for them. When the man had gone tramping off into the main building Steven turned away from the door and closed it, and found MacGuire shivering in his inadequate dressing-gown.

'Everything I've just said? I think so. Why?'

MacGuire moved his big feet up and down, clenching his arms across his chest. Their black hairs stood out from the goose-pimples. 'You mentioned adultery.'

'Did I?'

MacGuire said, 'I'm not sure.'

'If I did, I'll stick to it. It's true.' He looked round as if for a physical escape, having had enough of talking to this man. 'We'd better sit on that bench, with our feet up. Just because there's a smallpox epidemic it doesn't mean we can't still catch pneumonia.'

They went solemnly across to the bench and sat on it, drawing their dressing-gowns round them and hugging their knees. But silence was worse.

Looking at MacGuire he said: 'I suppose I've just been given confession. It was good of you, Father. As you're so fond of saying, it did me good. I'm sorry there's no penitence, only regret.' He waited for MacGuire to say something, but he did not. 'I don't mean I regret doing it. I'm just sorry that it was done.'

MacGuire sat like a monk, facing him, his eyes in this poor light looking like black holes in his shining face.

'It would be very handy if we could wipe out our footprints as we go along, yes.'

'Even burning my bridges would have lent the thing a little drama, but it wasn't necessary. I'm sorry for the man, that's all. Not for my wife because she doesn't know about it and it doesn't affect her, doesn't *diminish* her. I'm talking quite normally, aren't I?'

'Quite normally.'

'I'm sorry for the man because it's hit him where it hurts.' He looked at MacGuire and said without derision, 'My training has taught me that a man's more vulnerable between the legs than in his soul.'

MacGuire said nothing. He sat attentively as if he wished to learn from the other.

'I found out this evening that he knew about this, you see. He simply asked me: had I?'

The door banged open and an ambulance man came in, a thin, bright-faced, stalky-looking man, his eyes everywhere, his presence exploded against the bleak monastic scene.

'You'll catch your death in here, you will.' He was leaning backwards under the pile of clothes until they got up from the bench and helped him. 'You'll never recognise them, I'm afraid. It knocks the life out of them. You'll be lucky if nothing's got shrunk.'

He helped them put their clothes on to the bench, busying himself, an impromptu valet. 'Only one tie. Where's the other tie?'

Steven found his underclothes and began pulling them on.

'I don't very often sport a tie,' said MacGuire.

'You don't?' Then he saw the collar and jerked a surprised look at the priest. 'Well I never!' He stood back from them as they dressed. 'We're waiting for another one, aren't we? Did you come up here to see him, then?'

MacGuire buttoned his trousers, his large bare feet splaying out at the bottom, bone-white in contrast with the black trouser-legs.

'The boy?' he said.

'A kiddie, is it?' The pert face changed, the cheeks hollowing as the mouth tightened. He turned away. 'When's it going to end, eh?' He opened the door. 'When's it going to end?'

In the doorway he stood for a moment to light a cigarette. The flare of the match bloomed against the dark outside and silhouetted his thin neck and shoulders.

'Welford.'

'Yes, Doctor?'

'May I have one of those?'

The man came in again, fishing out the packet, the tinfoil glittering in the light.

'It's your last one.'

'That's okay.'

'You'll see my car outside the stores door. There's a packet on the seat, in front.' He took the cigarette. Welford struck a match for him.

'I shan't get no more chance for a bit. I smoke too many as it is.'

'We all do. Thanks.'

'You're welcome, Doctor.'

MacGuire put his jacket on and stood looking down at himself in the crumpled suit. The sides of the black jacket hung away from him like short wings.

'I look like a corpulent penguin,' he said mildly.

The ambulance man blew out cigarette-smoke in a gusty comment. 'It's a night for fancy dress, all right.' He left them, banging the door shut after him.

MacGuire laced his shoes. Their black leather was cracked across the uppers. 'And what did you answer?'

Steven thought of Preston's short-sighted eyes watching his face, the glasses in his hand.

'I told him I had,' he said.

'Why didn't you lie?'

'Because there was good reason to. I make a practice of telling lies only when there's not much point in it – just to bolster the social graces, you know. For an adulterous atheist I've got very high principles.'

He rested the cigarette on the edge of the bench while he put on his tie. MacGuire was brushing himself down with his hands, and said in a moment: 'He has asked me for advice.'

'Who has?'

'The man you have wronged.'

Steven remembered that Preston was a Catholic.

'How long have you known about this?'

'Some while.' He looked down as the cigarette rolled from the edge of the bench, disturbed by the draught of their movements. He bent and picked it up, nipping it gently between finger and thumb. Steven hesitated and then took it from him, looking up into his face.

'That was kind of you.' He felt a rare moment of humiliation. 'And what have you advised him?'

'I said I would talk to you.'

'That wasn't advice.'

'I said I would talk to you before advising him.'

'I see.' He put his jacket on and felt in the pockets. Everything had been put back into one pocket, and he began distributing his lighter, pen, keys and loose change among the others, saying to MacGuire: 'Now that you've talked to me, what will you advise him?'

'I am still unsure.'

'Oh.' He looked round the bare room. 'Perhaps there'll be another time, to talk. There's a lot of work for me to do in the town. I ought to be down there. I know you won't think me rude or disinterested.' He opened the door. 'Can I give you a lift?'

'Thank you.'

In the doorway Steven said: 'It's a pity, isn't it, that a disinfection room can only cleanse the surface of us?'

MacGuire lumbered out with him, into the smell of damp coke and soaking trees. 'To anyone else I would say, there's always a church open somewhere.' The mist was in their faces. It had come again to lie along the valley and there was the scent of woodsmoke in it from the chimneys in Wrexford Vale.

'The car's round this corner.' Their footsteps were sharp-sounding along the concrete path.

Sitting in the front of the car with him, Father MacGuire said: 'It's difficult for this man to know best what he should do. He feels for you and for your marriage. He's known you and your wife for many years.'

They drove down the East Road towards the gates.

'It's kind of him, but I hardly deserve his thought.'

'He thinks more of you than perhaps you do yourself. He feels very strongly that he should talk this over with your wife, when she is well again.'

The tyres hissed on the wet macadam surface, accentuating the enormous silence of the night, of which Steven was suddenly conscious. There was a hearse waiting outside the gates; it was as far as it was allowed to come. Two men stood about, their cigarettes glowing. The mist gave a soft grey bloom to the cellulose.

It would have looked like this for Julie. The hearse, the waiting men, and soon the rumble of the trolley coming down from the building, bringing her coffin to be handled by men in grotesque clothing, visored and shrouded for fear she should contaminate them. He had imagined, during the long sleepless nights, this scene for Julie, and had not looked at her bed or her things in the wardrobe because they would have sharpened the image of his desolation.

But she would be coming back to the house, to sit at the window and comb her hair, to lie among the bedclothes in the first grey light of the morning with her closed-eyed face turned towards him on the pillow, foxing him while he watched her, thinking she was still asleep.

He turned the windscreen wipers on; their blades made two fan-shapes on the misted glass.

'He feels he must tell my wife that I've been unfaithful. Is that what you mean?'

'Yes.'

'I'm not a friend of his, but I've known him a long time. He's not a vengeful man. I don't understand.'

MacGuire sat forward on the seat, gazing through the windscreen, bracing his bulk as they turned a corner. 'I can think of no way of telling you,' he said, his voice worried by the problem. 'No way of communicating. You see, you have violated his marriage, which was sacred to him. So he would like to do what he can to save yours, by removing the barrier that is between you and your wife.'

The road and the street-lamps seemed unreal, and the car moved through the mist automatically, isolated, a machine bearing them along a given course. The only reality was this fantastic situation, its huge shape still undefined, as mystic as the block of stone from which the sculptor must hammer out the truth.

'He believes it would save my marriage, does he?'

'Yes. I also believe it. But I haven't the right, as he has, to take any action. I can only advise him, since he has asked for my guidance.' He folded his hands on his knees.

'I broke into his house, so naturally he has the right to break into mine.'

'Not quite that——'

'It is exactly that. I'm not objecting. It's jungle logic, and I accept it——'

'You broke into his house to ravish his wife——'

'I do hope we can keep this on a serious level, Father. I'm liable to be amused at the idea of my wrenching at the front door with a jemmy and rushing upstairs to pin the woman screaming to the bed. In cold fact we met in London by mutual consent and shared a very civilised dinner before retiring discreetly to an anonymous hotel bedroom.

MacGuire waited, then said: 'It wasn't I who introduced the simile of house-breaking.'

'That's true. It wasn't. I chose a bad phrase.'

'A good one, I think. However civilised your sin, it was still a spiritual plundering of this man's house. Yet the right it gives him to invade yours isn't just by the law of an eye for an eye. He is entering your house for good purposes, as a friend. If your marriage were harmed, as well as his own, he would feel he had failed to do something about it.'

Steven drove slowly, crawling along the misty street. His skull shrank at the problem, the nerves drawing his scalp tight as if his head must be helped physically to contain the riot of thought before it could explode and overwhelm him. He must defend himself against this holy blackmail.

'So he wants to tell my wife, and "remove the barrier" – those were the words? I take it you mean the natural reserve of privacy between two people who spend their lives together——'

'There is no need for privacy——'

'In your belief. To my mind the idea of complete intimacy between two human beings is suffocating and undignified. Must they clean their teeth in front of each other and leave the lavatory door open? Without privacy there's no respect. Quite honestly I don't see what's in Preston's mind, unless it's petty vengeance, and that would surprise me, in him.'

MacGuire stared through the rhythmic fanning of the wiper-blade in front of him. There must be a way of communicating with this man, of making him see that human behaviour was not always suspect. But it was difficult, as difficult as trying to teach a strange language without one single common word to start with. He cleared his throat unhappily.

'He believes,' he said slowly, choosing simple words, 'that there can be no real substance in your marriage – no real trust, or companionship – while this secret lies between you and your wife. You can't open your heart or mind to her, in case she catches a glimpse of your infidelity. You can't speak freely to her without sometimes watching your words and having to remember not to mention a certain evening, a certain place, in case you make a slip, and are confused. He believes that this secret is a barrier, and that he has the right to bring it down for your sake. But of course he might be wrong, and that's why he has asked for my guidance.'

Over the glass of the windscreen the wipers argued together, flicking across and across and touching and sweeping away and coming back to the argument. Their sound got on the nerves, and Steven turned them off, and said to MacGuire:

'What does he want me to do?'

'I don't understand.'

'He threatens to hurt my wife and embarrass me by exposing an affair that's best forgotten. What does he want me to do? What's his price? I've wronged him, indirectly, and I admit it, and I'm prepared to bargain with him. What are his terms?'

'You are beginning to understand——'

'I'm glad. It can't be that complicated. I want to work out this before she comes home. I don't intend to let anyone make her unhappy now that she's coming back to life, but it's pretty clear to me that you're not going to dissuade him from busting in and wrecking our chances for the future. If he's insistent about it, I'd rather tell her myself.'

MacGuire's head turned to look at him. At the edge of his vision he was aware of its big dark shape and the gleam of the watching eyes. The voice was gentle and relieved. 'You understand, at last.'

'I do? What do I understand?'

'That those would be his terms.'

SEVEN

Three days later the mist became serious. Settling along the whole of the valley, as it did each year at this time, it blotted out the town and made travelling difficult between Kingsbourne and neighbouring districts. There had been spring rain and spring sunshine for weeks, and the moisture was rising and gathering, drifting between the hills and along the river's course. At night, drivers on the London road met layers of good visibility stretching for many yards, and sometimes drove with the top of the windscreen just below a vapour-layer until the dense whiteness bannered down and engulfed them, so that they must brake hard and dim their lights. They soon learned that there was no point in going faster through the clear patches, for they were few and short.

Cars had been moving in, tonight, from Wrexford Vale and Cookham, answering the emergency call from the Kingsbourne Health Department that had gone out before dark. The car park opposite the Town Hall was full but never still, for the investigation teams were coming and going, and the glass doors of the building had been bolted open for easy access to the main hall. The mist crept in, yellowing the lights and bringing dankness.

The day-shift of the department had gone off at seven o'clock, and Dr. Tewson had stayed until nearly midnight. It was now two in the morning and his deputy was in charge of operations – Claude Boswell, a thin, quiet man with a large head and little hair on it. His white skin, bald head and the thick pebble-glasses he wore gave him the unpleasant look of a creature that had come from beneath a big stone. His laugh did not help; it had nothing to do with mirth but exploded every so often and was accompanied by a nervous wrinkling of the eyes. If it was a nervous laugh it was incongrous, for he was not a nervous man. If he had been asked to explain this habit he would most probably have said: 'I expect I do it to jolly them all along.'

With Claude Boswell in the general administration rooms were two other medical officers: Canning, the smallpox consultant from the Ministry, and little Beesdale, the M.O. of the County Council. Beesdale, nearly sixty years old, spent his time hopping like a robin round a gardener, checking the lists before the clerks had got them off the duplicator, worrying the switchboard girls, pecking at each new problem as it arose and quite often solving it before the others had time to realise it was there. If anyone were jollying them along it was Beesdale, without the help of a bright-toothed laugh.

At this hour and in this situation pressure was high and tempers becoming edgy, though there had been no first-class row in here for days.

Boswell had said: 'Emotions are inefficient. If anyone wants to emote anything he can go and do it in the cloakrooms, not in here.' His laugh spluttered forth.

But they liked him. Most of them preferred him to Tewson, whose plodding precision made them impatient to get on with the job.

Sanders, the deputy chief sanitary inspector, had looked in twice tonight, flourishing lists. Nobody knew very much about Sanders, because he was new; but if they wanted a list, he'd have it.

The switchboard was working the whole time, with three girls trying to sift urgent calls from time-wasters. For every half-dozen appeals from worried mothers and elderly hypochondriacs there was one essential call from the police department of some town to which a contact had been known to have returned, or from the health department of a London borough with queries or information.

London was well on the Kingsbourne map and many of the calls were from there. An observation barrier had been thrown across the western suburbs by the County and the Metropolitan police forces because there had been cases of primary contacts leaving Kingsbourne on urgent personal business in London, exposing the capital's eight million population to epidemic risk.

Activity today had been exceptional. The volcano on which the Health Department had been sitting for nearly two weeks had now erupted: six cases of smallpox had broken out in various parts of the town among the people who had been under ob-servation since it was known they had become contacts. There was no problem with them: at the first sign of symptoms they had been examined and removed to the Kingsbourne Hospital and the Burford Isolation Hospital ten miles away. But five other new cases cropped up during the same period, and it was not until the evening that investigation showed the same source of infection: the Royalty Cinema.

It was thirteen days since Dolly Williams had been taken ill, and nine days since she had died.

As the reports had come in to the department, one or two people of the volunteer staff had become worried. They had asked the M.O.H. how far he expected this new outbreak to spread. Tewson had turned red eyes on them, thought carefully, and answered: 'There was an audience of thirteen hundred

73

people that evening. Not many of them would have been protected by recent vaccination, in those early days. On the other
hand, one usherette doesn't come into contact with more than a
tenth of the full audience, at this particular cinema. So there
were roughly a hundred and thirty primary contacts leaving the
cinema and going home to their families, or going to cafés for a
late coffee, or going back to their hotels in buses or taxis and
saying good-night to friends there. The cafés would be crowded,
and the buses and taxis crowded and busy, with the audiences
of four cinemas pouring out, with people still on their way home
from pubs and visits to friends and relations, from the theatre,
from whist-drives, bridge-parties, from the two dance-halls.'

His red eyes had gazed calmly at the worried members of the
volunteer staff. 'In short, this new outbreak isn't likely to spread
eventually over more than a hundred thousand people – which
is the estimated population of Kingsbourne as yet unprotected
by vaccination. If Mr. Simmonds has finished with the tray I
should be glad of some more coffee.'

But the figure by nightfall was only fifteen cases. There were
hopes that it wouldn't reach twenty. But there was nothing to
stop it rising to tragic proportions, except the work of these
people who were now, at two in the morning, busy in their
offices and along the streets, searching the town for the deadly
virus and where they could not kill it, isolate it.

Three new cases had come in before midnight, raising the
figure to eighteen. With the third case came a problem. There
was no known source of infection. At the house in Bewlay Road,
a doctor and two sanitary inspectors were questioning the
woman who lay in her bed waiting for the ambulance. Her mind
was clear but she could not say where she had been, thirteen days
ago – or ten days, or fifteen. She kept no diary. She had paid no
regular visits to friends or relations. She might have been any
where – but of one thing she was certain. She had not been to
any cinema for over a month.

'It's not a Royalty,' Beesdale said. He worried his moustache.
'It's a new one, from nowhere.'

The telephone near the main door was ringing again and he
answered it and came back to Boswell. 'They've taken her away
by ambulance to Burford. There isn't a fresh clue.'

'They'll never reach Burford in this fog. Why Burford?'

'Allocations, allocations.'

Boswell stared at the map through his pebble-lenses and said:
'It's a missed case.' He went on staring at the map while Beesdale
trotted away to the telephone again. Somewhere on the map was
either a crossed line or infection as yet untraced, or a carrier
moving, or a missed case.

'Dr. Boswell?'

74

He turned round and saw the editor of the *Kingsbourne Gazette*.

'My God, are you still up, Mr. Gracey?'

'Can we help?'

'Help?'

'What can we publish?'

Boswell looked at the map again. 'Idle gossip from foreign sunshine resorts, a review of the Test, and plenty of comic cartoons, if you want my prescription.'

Gracey picked at his ear. 'They don't want to escape. They want to be told. What shall we tell them?'

Boswell turned and looked at him again, staring at the street-names and infection-foci flags that were superimposed on the editor's face below the ruff of ginger hair. 'Tell them?'

'They'll want to know.' Gracey's outline was blurred, and the Deputy M.O.H. blinked energetically. He had come on the night-shift two hours ago but he had been on the day-shift as well.

'To know? Of course. If you're right, that is. Tell them that this new outbreak was expected and that we have been awaiting it. Don't add of course that this fact won't help us in the slightest.'

The editor watched the bright-toothed laugh, and when it was over, said: 'We'll run a special. The Health Department pouncing on this new threat the moment it emerges.'

'Like a cat at a mousehole?'

'You feel like a cat at a mousehole?'

'I feel like a rather stringy length of waterlogged rope. How do you feel, Mr. Gracey?'

'I'm all right. There's news about. What happened to Mr. Buckridge?'

'A nervous breakdown.'

'A bad one?'

'There is no such thing. A nervous breakdown is an admirable institution. It's when you don't have one that you come apart at the seams.'

'Will he be back here?'

'Tomorrow, if Mrs. Buckridge will allow him. She's a forceful soul, and a wicked hand at bridge, as I know to my cost. Now if you will excuse me . . .'

'We say that you have the situation under control, for the very good reason that you expected it and had made exhaustive arrangements to meet it. All right?'

'Yes. "Exhaustive" in big capitals.'

He watched Gracey going down between the desks, his back covered with street-names and infection-foci flags.

Somewhere in the town, a missed case. He heard himself muttering, and looked round to see if anyone were watching him.

It wouldn't do to mutter, or nibble a nail, or let the voice rise. Buckridge's voice had gone up and up until he had suddenly said: 'It's beating us. What are we going to do? It's beating us. They had found him drinking tea at a bus-garage at six in the morning and he had told them he couldn't come back.

'Admiralty again, sir.'

Serve him right for being such a tough little nut. It never worked, unless you were born one.

'What do they want?'

'Confirmation of details. They're having the full crew of H.M.S. *Tricker* vaccinated and quarantined.'

Somewhere in the town, a missed case. The girl had a thin shiny face and unimaginative eyes. *Bewlay Road* was printed across her forehead. She watched him uneasily.

'Where is *Tricker*?'

'Gib, sir.'

'What?'

'Gibraltar.'

'Ask Mr. Frisard to give you the details. When you've done that, get Dr. Scott-James and Dr. Monks on the phone for me in that order. You'll have to ring for a long time. They're in bed.'

'Yes, sir.'

He reminded her of a man who had once followed her all the way home from school, a tall man with a large white head and thick glasses that had flashed in the afternoon sunlight past the sweet-shop windows. It couldn't have been Dr. Boswell, but it reminded her, and she felt afraid of him.

Her hair bobbed away from him and he stood still in front of the map on the wall. How could people be so ignorant that you had to go and fetch them out of their homes and put them into hospital? Couldn't they telephone and say they had 'flu symptoms, a pain in the small of the back, shivering, vomiting? Didn't they know there was an epidemic in the town?

'Someone taken ill at the Gate House.' Beesdale was back, pert and busy. 'The third.'

'Who's there?'

'Matthews and Clarkson. We've passed it on to Sanders.'

'Beesdale.'

'Yes?'

'There's a missed case.'

'Sanders is working on that. He's been working on it for two hours.'

'We've *all* got to work on it.'

'We're all working on it.'

'I suppose we are.'

The wrinkles across Beesdale's forehead ran from one temple

to the other in perfectly-spaced curves as he looked up at Boswell and said, 'You've drunk too much coffee.'

Bennett had called on Extension 26 half an hour ago and was on his way back. Three other inspectors were covering the Bewlay Road case and the two latest 'Royalties' while the main team was reporting by telephone at every thirty minutes, drawing blank wherever they went. But they sent lists in, and the figure for primary contacts of the 'Royalty' cases had gone up to a hundred and nine by three o'clock.

Coker had telephoned from Wrexford. It had taken him nearly forty minutes to drive there through the mist in search of a primary, a woman who had given birth to a child yesterday morning.

'It's got scars,' he said. He was put through to the Deputy M.O.H.

'The baby has scars?' Boswell asked.

'Yes. Not bad ones.'

'They look like smallpox marks?'

'They could be. I wouldn't be certain.'

'Who is the woman's doctor?'

'Dr. Challick, in the village here.'

Boswell telephoned Dr. Challick.

The message had come back a few minutes ago. The mother was beginning the predromal rash and was being put into an ambulance sent from King's. The child had been through the disease while still in the womb, and the scars were not serious.

Collins had phoned from the other side of the town, drawing blank on the missed case. He was out of petrol.

Sanders was down at the Sanitary Inspectorate switchboard himself with headphones and mouthpiece on. He sat surrounded by his lists. They were coming in faster than he could check them, but there was no quicker way. He was on the line now to the Crossings Hotel, five miles up the London road.

Dr. Scott-James had come into Boswell's office with a scarf and mackintosh covering his pyjama-top, a pair of pin-striped trousers on, and his golf-shoes. Four hours ago he had walked into a ditch when his team had abandoned their car on the other side of the railway, where the Wrex was flooding its banks at Leylands Farm.

'If these bloody things get soaked as well I've got my gum boots in reserve. What's the excitement now?'

'There's a missed case.'

'God help us. Where's the coffee?' His stubble was grey in the lights.

Someone came in and said: 'Dr. Beesdale's just going out to Shipton Lane, sir. There's someone ill there.'

'Mowbray? Is the name Mowbray?'

'Yes, sir.'

'They've sent out to there already——'

'The car ran into a street island in the fog——'

'Is anyone hurt?'

'No, sir.'

'Have you seen Dr. Monks here yet?'

'He's just come in, sir.'

'Is there any coffee left?'

'I'll see, sir.'

Scott-James said: 'Where do you find these girls?'

'I don't know. They come and volunteer.'

'They're a lively lot.'

'Aren't you too old for lechery by now?'

'The older you get the worse it is. Didn't your mother tell you?'

Boswell got a line through to Sanders' office and was answered by his assistant. Mr. Sanders was on the switchboard at present. Would Mr. Sanders please ring him as soon as possible?

Scott-James lit a cigarette. 'You've got me out of my bed, Claude old son. What do I do now – sit on my backside?'

'They're tracing as hard as they can. Have you got any petrol in your car?'

'Yes, and who's going to pay for it? She'll be due for a rebore by the time this lot's over.'

'Didn't you put in a claim?'

'Nobody told me.'

The telephone on the desk rang and Boswell picked it up as someone came in and Scott-James said: 'Good old Monkey. Boswell wants us for a sunbeam.'

Steven looked at them, squinting in the light. He had shaved half his face, cut it badly, and stopped.

'You want an electric. They fairly buzz it off.'

'Hasn't buzzed yours off, much.'

'I didn't have time. The Health Department Under-Secretary for Clandestine Affairs was twittering fit to cause a short-circuit on the phone. How's Julie?'

'Over the worst.' His face was sore where he had cut it. He had begun to dread her coming home, because he would have to keep his word and tell her, and it would be a stupid thing to do, a harmful one. Yet he didn't believe he could talk Preston out of it. 'What do they want us here for?'

'To impress their friends and influence people.'

Boswell talked to Sanders on the telephone until a tray of coffee came in, with cracked cups, a single dented aluminium spoon, a bowl of granulated sugar with tea-coloured coagulated lumps among it, and no saucers.

Scott-James began pouring out his coffee, his face pensive

about its colour. 'It's never been near a coffee-bean,' he said. 'It's been near a good many unwholesome things in its time, but never a genuine bean.'

Steven leaned his buttocks against the window-sill and watched Boswell. The receiver looked out of proportion gripped in that big hairless hand.

'It smells like a deodorant,' said Scott-James. 'Have a cup?'

'Not just now.' He was still on Dexedrine. He wandered to the mirror above the calendar and peered into it to see if his cheek were still bleeding. It had stopped and the blood had caked to a blob; but it would only start again if he were to pick it off. He turned away from the mirror and heard Boswell say:

'And not a Sombrero contact?'

Julie had been one of those. They had made her believe now that it was modified; she knew now that she wasn't going to die. She had been very calm about it when he had gone to see her yesterday. Was she doubtful about her reception when she could come home? Was he still going to be in a strange bitter mood – and was it in some way her fault? He had tried to put her mind at ease, by talking to her as he had used to talk before this obsession had surfaced in him. He would never, in any case, see Ruth alone again. He would leave her to the others whom he had never met nor even heard of, but of whose existence he was always certain.

'. . . From any known source of infection,' Boswell was saying, and in a moment put the receiver down. Scott-James was drinking coffee and had poured out a cup for Boswell, leaving it on the desk. There was a faint rainbow film on the surface of it. 'The Crossings Hotel,' Boswell said. 'They have a man ill there. Bennett's gone down to find a spare car.' He looked at each of them and Steven said:

'All right.'

'I got here first,' said Scott-James. His cup was still full, the coffee too hot to drink quickly. Steven looked at it and said:

'You'd better finish that muck. I had some before I came out.' He looked at Boswell. 'That's up the London road, at the R.A.C. box. Does Bennett know how far it is?'

'If you know the way, that's all that matters. You can tell him. The people there sound rather weird, Sanders tells me, but from what he can gather the man's very ill, so we'll do what we can to raise an ambulance to follow. But telephone, of course.'

'I will.'

'But why in God's name,' Boswell appealed to them, 'don't people report an illness earlier, with an epidemic on? *Why*?'

'Because it takes all sorts to make a world,' Scott-James said, 'and it's mostly the other sort. Good hunting, Monkey.'

When Steven went out the clock on the wall said a quarter past three.

.   .   .   .

The other car hit them a few hundred yards short of the cross-roads, five miles out of Kingsbourne up the London arterial. It happened in a patch of good visibility.

There had been three or four of these clear patches, but Bennett had not put on speed through them. He had driven on this road at this time of the year before, and knew that to accelerate through a clear patch was to run into the mist again faster than was safe; and on this road the limit of safety was reached at fifteen or twenty miles an hour.

Starting out from Kingsbourne, Steven had been silent but Bennett had begun a dissertation on the short-comings of the Health Department's administration, and Steven had sometimes listened, sometimes let him run on without his attention. To a man like Bennett, who was a town councillor and chief whip of the local Conservative Association's jamboree programme, it did not matter who listened or who declined to listen. The wise would be sure to hear and understand; the others were not important.

'In a word, they lack co-ordination.' He gave the word emphasis on the hyphen; the wise could even deduce the Latin root of a word if they wished, from this meticulous pronunciation. 'On the one hand you see half the Inspectorate working brilliantly, and the other half beating the air for guidance; on the other hand you see half the staff of the Medical working hard to liaison with the useless half of the Inspectorate, and the other half beating the air.'

Steven stopped listening at this point, having lost the score of hands and halves. He sat watching the white wall of the mist in front of them and wondered how long Bennett had possessed a licence.

'Saunders is all *right*, but he's *new*.'

'You know this road pretty well?'

'What? Yes. Like the back of my hand. You see, Buckridge is a case in point. He's had a nervous breakdown simply because he took it on himself to run the whole show from the top instead of decentralising and delegating – mark you, I've a suspicion he *realises* there's no co-ordination inside the Department, and is *obliged* to assume full responsibility on every level. Even Sanders might have divined that much, because he's taken over sole charge of the switchboard himself. But it's not enough for the chief of a department to turn himself into a one-man band.'

Steven listened to the wipers, the drone of the engine, the flutter of air past the window-louvre and Bennett's voice. It was a steady, lulling voice, and pleasant to hear. A child would recognise instinctively the tone of a great teacher, and would

listen under its spell without learning, and would grow up to
believe he was a dunce because nothing would seem to have sunk
in.

'. . . As well as *industry*, there has to be administration. I tried
to put this particular point across to Buckridge, only a few
months ago, but . . .'

The mist was a white blank. They were driving through milk.
Buckridge had a nervous breakdown because he had turned on
the pressure too suddenly, that was all. Afraid of not doing
enough. If there were any lack of co-ordination in his department
it was his own doing.

'. . . One of mine?'

'Yes.' The chances of its being the right answer were fifty-fifty.

'Help yourself.'

'What?'

Bennett opened the glove-pocket on the dashboard and took
out the packet of cigarettes.

'Oh. Thanks.'

They lit up and Steven wound the window down to let the
smoke out. 'I'd say it's about another half-mile.'

He noticed Bennett check the speedometer-trip with a down-
ward glance. 'A fraction more, actually.'

You wouldn't catch Bennett napping.

Steven automatically registered the set of the needle at just
above twenty-five as the white glow inside the car was dimmed.
There was less reflection on the mist from the spotlamp; they were
running into a clear patch. Bennett didn't speed up.

'The same fault lies like a weak stratum of rock, right through
the Civil Service.'

The mist broke up and small clouds of it drifted past the beam
of the spotlamp. They could make out trees, and the gleam of
the cats'-eyes in the roadway. Then the image of the other car
was suddenly on the windscreen as if flashed there by a film-
projector, its shape expanding as it neared, its lights burning into
Bennett's eyes as he brought the wheel over and Steven threw an
arm round the back of his seat to stop himself being shot forward
against the dashboard when the impact came.

It came as a soft grinding tear as the metal bodies glanced and
the door handles were ripped away. The car was rocking on its
soft springs and Bennett put his foot on the throttle to give it
the power to pull out of the slide that was taking them over the
grass verge towards a telegraph pole. The nearside front wheel
hit a hummock and they bounced before the rear end broke away
and the car slewed through ninety degrees and stopped at the
base of the pole.

Bennett turned the ignition off.

'You all right?'

'Yes. Listen.'

From the invisible night there came a high-pitched storm of sound that held them rigid. Their imagination had to find its identity and for a few seconds it was not easy . . . it was like a siren's blast . . . or the transmission-whine of a lorry approaching. . . .

'He's turned over,' Bennett said. 'Come on!'

They got out and ran back along the road towards the wall of mist and the hellish sound that loudened as they neared. Glass shattered musically and then the sound ran on alone, guiding them.

They found the car straddling the ditch on its side. Steven felt a pattering against his legs but did nothing about it as he stumbled half-way into the ditch and found the windows. One was shattered, the other still whole. He hit it with his fist and the glass broke away into snowy granules, falling into the car.

Bennett shouted – 'Switch that bloody engine off!'

Steven could see nothing inside the car. He swung up and hitched himself on to the door pillar and then lowered his body through the smashed window very carefully; but his legs touched nothing alive. The back of the car was empty. Shut in with the dreadful sound, he groped forward and felt the rim of the steering-wheel and then the dashboard. A bunch of keys were dangling. He turned them against their ring and the ring turned the key that was in the ignition lock.

His eardrums slowly expanded as the noise began dying away in a long slow cadence. The trembling of the bodywork stopped. There was a reek of hot oil, and a scent he couldn't define.

'. . . In there?' Bennett was shouting again.

'What?' Steven levered himself upright, poking his head and shoulders out. The white blob of Bennett's face loomed. 'There's nobody inside. Have a look around. They were thrown clear.'

Bennett went splashing about in the ditch, calling 'Where are you? Where are you?' The water was up to his knees. It hadn't been his fault. Monks would be able to say they were well over on their own side, and not going fast. 'Where are you?' The mist came by them in cold white drifts.

Steven climbed down to the grass and moved round the car, poking underneath in case there was anyone in the hollow beneath it. The warmth of the axle and couplings was against his face. He managed to fit a small mystery into the pattern of facts: the car had stayed in gear, and when it had turned on its side the rear wheels had been freed and had spun fast to the jammed throttle; so the pattering against his legs must have been mud slinging off the tyre as it churned into the soft wet grass.

Bennett came dodging out of the water. 'I'm going to bring the car back and use the lights.' His footsteps went padding away down the road. Steven felt his way down into the water and crawled under the car, coming out on the other side and then trudging down the length of the ditch for a dozen yards, coming back to round the car and search the water for the same distance on the other side.

A faint glow dawned, blanching the dark, and he could hear Bennett's engine nearing. The scene took on details: the flat glint of water, the green of the banks and hedgerow, a gate, the brown flint at the roadside shining. He turned back and saw the silhouette of the overturned car against Bennett's headlights.

'Have you found anyone?' The door slammed and Bennett came into view.

'No. They're not under the water. I've looked.'

They began working along the bottom of the hedge, covering the oblong area formed by the banks of the ditch.

'Listen.'

The mist swirled past the headlamp beams.

'What?' asked Bennett in a moment.

'I thought I heard someone.'

They waited again in silence. The joints of the engine made small cracking sounds as it began cooling. There was nothing else.

'Have you got a torch in your car?'

Bennett clambered out of the ditch and went to fetch it. Steven stood listening. He had thought he heard the sound of a human, of a voice, inarticulate, so short-lived that his memory had no time to register or discriminate between a sob or word. Logic could suggest only that it was a sound of pain, if there really had been one at all.

The beam of the torch came lancing through the mist and Steven said: 'Check up inside.'

They moved in to the car and peered down through the smashed windows. The back seat was cocked across the space. In the front, chocolates had spilled from a dark blue box and were scattered over the door panel. The keys were still swinging on their metal ring. The gear-lever was bent downwards from the steering-column. Flecks of blood gleamed on the rim of the wheel, and had it not been for them Steven could almost have believed the car had been driverless when it had crashed.

He said: 'They were hurt.'

'Yes. They couldn't have been thrown out. They must have climbed out through here. But where the devil . . . ?'

'Stolen, I think,' Steven said.

'What?'

'They've cleared off.'

'They must be somewhere——'

'We've looked——'

'Not everywhere——'

'We've called out.'

Bennett drew his head from the window-space and switched off the torch. 'They're hurt. Unconscious.'

'They climbed out.'

Bennett gestured, frustrated. 'And then ran a bit, and lost consciousness. 'You're a doctor – you know it could happen.'

Steven stood back from the car, aware of the chill of his soaked clothes for the first time. Wearily he said: 'My common sense tells me that they've cleared off. I'd say it's a stolen car, batting along at this time of night.'

'Well, I'm going to go on searching.' There was a note of heroic stamina in Bennett's voice.

'You go on searching, and I'll walk on to the Crossings Hotel. It's not far now. I'll ring the police from there and they can take over from you.'

'They might be dying.'

Bennett was a man who liked company in his heroism.

'There's someone dying up at the hotel. I'll see to him first, since the other's not available.' He got his bag from the car.

Along the road he found he had developed a limp and reached down, finding blood in his shoe. He did not remember how it had happened. Climbing into the crashed car, perhaps, too intent upon finding the occupants to notice the jagged edges of the window-frames or the buckled metal of the pillar when he had swung his legs through.

He walked through the clear patch of wan starlight into the next wall of mist. There was a cross-roads and an R.A.C. box outside the grounds of the hotel. It should not be hard to find.

The night had cut him off from other people. He was alone, walking along a road through a desert of white oblivion. The last man in the world would find himself like this when all the others had gone. And probably in as bad a shape.

The porch smelt of mildew and rotting plants and was lit with the ghastly blue glow of a high lamp with coloured panes. A big iron knocker was rusted into uselessness, still raised from the plate of the door as if the last hand to lift it had hesitated and then decided not to call here after all. Then rain had brought the rust and made permanent the evidence of a change of mind.

'Who is it?'

The voice filled the confines of the porch, sharp and disembodied. A crack of light shone from the flap of the letterbox. Steven bent down and said: 'A doctor.'

The metal flap moved and he could see the edges of three dry white finger nails keeping it open against the spring. The voice had the horrible energy of a caged bird's.

84

'Is it Dr. Wilson? You are not Dr. Wilson.'

His legs were clamped by the chill of the soaked trousers. He was beyond impatience. The night would never end and he was part of it and so would live for ever in this fantasy.

He told the letter-box that his name was Monks and that he had been sent by the Kingsbourne Medical Officer of Health to attend someone here who was ill.

'This is the Crossings Hotel.' The announcement was automatic like a machine giving his weight and fortune.

Someone else was speaking now, inside the house. A younger voice and less sharp, though insistent. A muffled argument began. He waited. It was strangely difficult to re-enter the world of people.

Suddenly the door was dragged open with a shiver of bolts and light struck his eyes from flaring yellow candelabra; and the house was filled with barking. The eyes of dogs shone from the shadows of the hall.

A tall woman looked at him. She had grey hair and a violet dress and her teeth were long; the lips were pulled back from them in suspicion. The younger one was thin too but dressed in a brown shapeless garment like a housecoat: one would have the impression that this was her favourite and she had worn it for years and would never part with it. It was a shell. She had a pale pinched face and eyes full of hurt that looked out, narrowed, from an habitual flinch.

The barking of the dogs sent a brittle echo leaping round the walls. Above the din Steven asked:

'May I use your telephone?'

The two women stared at him and he realised his aspect. He was half-shaven and cut about the face and his clothes were soaked and muddied from the waist down. There was blood stiffening on his sock at the ankle. 'I'm sorry to appear like this. There's been an accident along the road.' He looked from the one to the other. They had drawn back from him, the mother's attitude shielding the daughter. The girl's eyes stared out from the shelter of the womb that she had never mentally left.

'An accident. . . . Are you hurt?'

Their eyes inspected him again while two of the dogs crept on their bellies towards him and then sprang away yelping when he moved towards the telephone on the hall-stand. 'No, I'm not hurt, thank you. There's another man on his way here, one of the sanitary inspectors from the Health Department.' It might save Bennett's having to shout through the letter-box.

He asked the operator for the Kingsbourne police, raising his voice above the barking of the dogs. They were creeping up to him again and as he stood facing the wall with the telephone in his hand he was struck with the sudden thought: Are *they*

85

moving nearer too?

He would rather the dogs than the women.

The police came on the line and he told them about the accident. There was no trace of the driver except a little blood on the steering-wheel. He was sorry not to have thought of getting the number of the car. An Esquire saloon, grey.

When he put the receiver down and turned round he saw they had not moved. The girl said daringly: '*We* have an Esquire saloon car.'

He nodded. 'They're very popular. I understand there is someone here who is ill. I should like to see him.'

They glanced at each other and for this moment he saw their faces in profile. The delineation was identical, and on it the husband and father had left no mark. The girl was a reflection of her mother. But when their heads turned again he could see the difference: strength in the older face, submission in the girl's. It seemed impossible to believe there had been a man in these two women's lives. There was no sign of him in this house of these faces.

'Mr. Bradley,' the mother said. 'He is upstairs.'

The barking began as they all moved, and his nerves were jarred by the din. There were four dogs, all of them small and of uncertain pedigree. The largest had matted fur and rheumy eyes; yellow teeth showed as it barked. Steven could smell its caries and accumulated dirt.

'I'll go,' the mother said. 'I'll go.' The girl hung back, leaning her thin arms on the newel post at the bottom of the stairs to watch them go up.

They stopped as a bell rang somewhere in the deeper reaches of the house and the girl swung round to look at the front door. Steven looked down at her and said: 'That will be my colleague.' His voice was drowned by the barking. The woman called in a clear high voice –

'Open the door, Clara!'

They stood watching the girl as she moved among the dogs. Steven saw Bennett's dishevelled legs below the glare of the candelabra. He was saying something to the girl and had difficulty in making himself heard; then he came inside and the dogs drew back, huddling, expressing their habitual distrust of any stranger. Steven wondered, did they learn it from the girl or she from them?

'I'm up here, Bennett.'

He came fully into Steven's view. He had to shout. 'Someone came along from a cottage near the car. They'd heard it. I asked them to look for the driver while I came on here.' He looked at the girl. 'They say the car belongs to this place. The Crossings Hotel.'

Steven felt the mother's agitation beside him on the stairs.

'From here? From *here*?' She began going down to look more closely at Bennett, who said:

'A grey Esquire saloon, 0454 SM.'

The girl swung round to look at her mother. 'It's ours. It's our car!'

The mother turned to stare up at Steven and her pale face cleared, dissolving to an embarrassed smile. 'How bewildering!'

'But, *Mummy* . . .'

'Tell William to go and find out. Tell William. *He'll* know.'

She came up the stairs again and Bennett followed her, first putting a hand down and brushing his fingers and thumb together as a gesture to the dogs. They scuffled away from him to bark from the safety of the shadows.

Steven's eardrums contracted painfully. The sound of his own voice filled his head. 'Please show me to Mr. Bradley's room.'

On the landing the woman stopped beside a bamboo and wicker cupboard and said earnestly: 'He is very ill, Doctor.'

'Yes.'

'We must be quiet.'

The barking sent echoes up the well of the stairs and they were trapped under the ceilings. The woman took Steven down a passage where a bulb burned inside a bead shade. He could hear Bennett behind them.

She tapped gently at a door and then opened it, standing aside with a gesture of modesty. 'Please go in. I'll wait for you downstairs.' She took one deliberate glance into the room and turned away, walking with quick dissembling strides down the passage.

Steven and Bennett went into the room. The light was on. It was a big square room with a high ceiling shadowed with dusty mouldings. A large double bed was pushed into one corner and its disproportion was accentuated by the tallboy and chest of drawers that were herded into the same corner to leave an expanse of faded carpet.

Electric flex trailed from a wall-plug to a bedside lamp whose parchment shade was cracked with a bright fissure. Bradley lay on the bed, half in the light and half in the feebler light of the ceiling lamp. He did not move, but stared upwards from a young dark face shining with sweat.

Steven put him at forty. People ill in bed always looked younger; their helpless dependence and sometimes their fear lent them the look of a child.

'How do you feel, Mr. Bradley?'

Bennett was moving around the room. The barking of the dogs had died away. The mist pressed white at the windows.

'Bad.'

Steven opened his bag. 'Feverish?'

87

With an effort the man asked: 'Have I got it?'

'I don't know what you've got.' He drew the bedclothes down. The pyjamas were soaked with sweat.

Bennett came and looked down at him. 'Can you answer a few questions, Mr. Bradley?'

Steven opened the pyjamas and said: 'Would you let me finish my examination first?'

'Go ahead.' He went wandering the room again. Steven moved to take his own shadow from the bed and found a rash on the man's stomach and inside his thighs. It was not yet umbilicated or spotty.

'Head aching?'

'Yes.'

'Where? At the front or back?'

'Front.'

Steven pulled the pyjamas together and put a thermometer into Bradley's mouth. 'Gently. Any pain in the back?'

'Yes.' Bradley had not looked at him but stared upwards all the time. 'Where's she gone?' He spoke as if praying.

'Where has who gone?'

The wrist was clammy under his finger. After a long time Bradley said: 'My wife.'

'I haven't seen her. I expect she's somewhere about. She's not ill?'

'No. But I've got it, haven't I?'

'You show some of the symptoms, but we'll catch it early. There's no real worry at this stage.' He took the thermometer out. It showed a hundred and three. He slipped it into the formalin envelope and quietly snapped it, putting it on to the windowsill. 'We'll get you to hospital and you can have a thorough check-up.'

He looked round to find Bennett. 'If you'd like to ask your questions. . . .' Moving away from the bed he murmured, 'But keep your distance.'

Closing his bag he listened to Bennett, who stood at the foot of the bed with his notebook.

'When did you visit Kingsbourne last, Mr. Bradley?'

'I can't remember.'

'It would be helpful if you tried. Was it within the past fortnight?'

Steven lifted the lid of a stained three-ply wash-closet and found the hand-basin. He began washing his hands in the lukewarm water, running it freely from the tap.

There was a thin oval piece of mauve soap.

'. . . From Ireland, a month ago.'

'But Kingsbourne?'

Rust came from the tap in small flakes. A door slammed

somewhere below in the house but the dogs did not bark again. His ankle was throbbing and he realised he was supporting much of his weight against the edge of the closet. The stimulant was wearing off. He straightened up.

'. . . The film with Jacquetta Lee? It was called "Beyond Uunderstanding". Can you remember?'

The pipes shuddered as the tap was turned off. An air lock went banging along them. He wiped his hands on his handkerchief, for there was no safe towel in this house now.

'. . . With anyone?' There was silence. 'Did you go alone, or with anyone?'

'My . . .'

'Yes? Your wife, Mr. Bradley?'

'No. Alone.'

Steven said quietly, 'I'll go down and telephone.'

Bennett came across to him, murmuring, 'A Royalty. Is he semi-delirious?'

'No. As bright as we are.'

Bennett looked at Steven's cothes and his own. 'How bright is that?' He went back to the foot of the bed, and as Steven turned towards the door he stopped. For a moment he felt as cut off from his surroundings as he had been along the road in the mist. There was only himself standing here with the same indefinable scent that he had noticed inside the crashed car. And the thin oval piece of mauve soap.

A pulse started beating in his temple. The room had gone cold and he listened to his own breathing. Bennett's voice was a distant drone from the other world.

The rear wheel of the car had spattered him with mud. The car had come from here, belonged to this house. The people at the cottage had told Bennett. It had just started out from here when it had crashed. It had started out half an hour after Sanders had telephoned the woman, saying he was sending a doctor to see the man who was ill.

There was nothing in this room but Bradley's; nothing of his wife's, except the piece of mauve soap.

He went back and lifted the lid of the wash-closet and looked down again at the thin oval, and remembered the other piece on the side of the wash-basin in the London hotel. Lowering the lid of the closet he went across to the bed.

'While you've been staying here, has your wife used the car?'

Bennett said: 'I'm not quite finished yet.' He looked at Steven's calm white face and did not understand the brightness of his eyes.

'Sometimes,' Bradley said, staring at the ceiling.

Bennett turned away impatiently, his reflection fleeting across the blank misty white of the window.

'What is your wife's first name?'

It was a handsome face on the pillow, dying with the youth still in it. 'Tell me if I've got the disease. I want to know.'

Steven watched the face. It had the dark wildness of features that would suit her taste.

'This woman . . . we'll call her your wife. Her name is Ruth, isn't it?'

For the first time Bradley looked away from the ceiling and up into Steven's eyes.

EIGHT

In the early morning the pine trees stood in a gold haze as the sun, coming above the hill, washed its light among their stems and along the cold ribbon of the road. There was no traffic, so early, nor would there be much when the day wore on. The town of Kingsbourne had become an island, and people did not go there if they could help it.

There were marks in the road where tyres had torn at the macadam; and ruts and bruises of fresh earth were dark on the grass where the car had overturned, almost opposite the cottage. Dr. Beesdale was knocking at the door. After a long time, during which he and the two other men stood under the mossy canopy of the porch blowing into their hands, a thin brown-faced man opened the door and looked at them with the calm of the country-man who has learned from the gale and deluge and drought to be surprised by nothing.

Beesdale apologised for calling so early. The man stared at him, placing him at once as a motorist out of petrol or with a puncture – moreover, one who had been driving all night long by the look of his white face and puffy eyes.

'Who came out to help with the motor-car last night?'

'The motor?' The bright eyes looked across the road; the brown rheumatic hand gestured derisively – 'That one?'

'Yes. The one that overturned.' Beesdale blew into his hands again. The morning was mild but he was cold from fatigue.

'I went across, that's right. Didn't see a smell of anyone, though.'

'You were looking for the driver.'

'Of course I was. But there wasn' one.'

'He had gone away,' nodded Beesdale. He sniffed at wood-smoke in the air, reminded of camping when he was a boy half a century ago with gold mornings like this one. 'He was lost in the mist.'

The man blinked up at the sun with the look on his face that it was a friend of his. 'I've found sheep in a mist, but I couldn' find him.'

The two men with Beesdale shifted their feet. With luck they'd be in bed before noon.

'You see,' Beesdale said, 'the driver of that car was a close contact of a smallpox case.'

'Oh, ay. We've heard a lot about that. It soun's bad.'

'Yes. Now did you look inside the car, or *get* inside it, when you were looking for the driver?'

The man turned away from the sun, smelling the warm soil. The ditches were blocked and half the low field still under water. They'd be lucky if a lot of the seed wasn't drowned and moulding. 'I searched about a bit,' he said.

'Did you get into the car, or look inside it through one of the windows?'

'That couldn'a been where he was, though.' He began looking badgered, and moved his feet back a few inches to the doorway. 'The man said. Told me.'

Beesdale felt his nose trying to drip and fished out his handkerchief. 'This is very important, you see——'

'He'd gone. Gone clean. No sign of a smell of him anywhere, an' I've found sheep under snow, many a time.'

The sanitary inspector with Beesdale put his hands behind him and wandered idly down the narrow brick path, to stand at the gate. Beesdale trumpeted briefly into his handkerchief and put it away.

'I must know,' he said, 'whether you actually got inside the car, or *looked* inside it, because——'

'The man *told* me. "They're not in the car still," he told me. So 't'was natural I shouldn't look in there for 'em.'

'So you didn't come into contact with the inside of the car?'

'I've said so.'

'You said it was natural, but——'

'Well if that isn' natural, what is, then? If this man *told* me there was nobody still inside the thing, then why should I go an' poke about? 'T'wouldn' be sense!'

Beesdale turned and looked at the sanitary inspector, who was standing at the gate as if he owned the place. Mr. Coker lived in a flat, and everyone knew he'd like a place of his own like this. He looked the part, gazing over the front gate with his hands behind him, the back of his trousers still warm, it might seem, from his own fireside.

'Because if you made any contact with the inside of that car,' said Beesdale, 'you stand the risk of catching the pox.'

'I'm a clean-livin' man.'

'As long as you understand the situation. It's a serious one.' But the man had turned and was shouting for someone in the house. Beesdale had started down the pathway, the St. John's volunteer with him.

'Alice!'

A woman called an answer from inside the house. Mr. Coker opened the gate and they filed through.

'What did ye do with them chocolates, Alice?'

92

Beesdale was busy with his nose again, and the St. John's volunteer said: 'They're bright, aren't they, down here in the sticks?'

Coker opened the door of his neat black Austin and started the engine. Beesdale was putting his handkerchief away. In a moment, as if he had been thinking it out, he turned his head and looked at the man in the doorway of the cottage. He could see only his thin brown face perched above the quickthorn hedge.

'Were there some chocolates in the car?' he called out, and the man nodded. The woman was now next to him in the doorway. Beesdale looked in through the open window of Coker's car and said: 'I think we've got a job on here. Bring my bag with you, there's a good chap.'

The sun was strong now although from the garage you could see the haze still across the trees and hedges where the land sloped to the valley. The haze was now blue, the first tint of a promised summer, the soft blue of the bloom on a grape. A church spire poked through it and the sun winked on the weather-vane.

An air-compressor throbbed at the back of the garage, its wire belt-guard quivering; a leak of air hissed through the joint of a grease-gun where the hose-clip was cutting into the rotting rubber. As Mr. Coker was speaking, the automatic cut-out flicked open and the compressor stopped, and his voice seemed suddenly loud in the silence.

'. . . when you towed it in. Who was steering it?'

'Alf,' the foreman said. Alf was a very tall man with overalls too short and his big feet were splayed out like a clown's. He wiped his hands constantly on a rag that was blacker than they.

'You drove, Alf?' asked Dr. Beesdale, and Alf nodded.

'Well, sat an' steered, like. We didn't start the engine because she'd lost a lot of oil when she went over, see?'

Mr. Coker eased his stubbly neck inside his collar. 'Were you the only one to get inside the car?'

'I think so. Bob might've took a look. I don't know.'

'It's very important,' said Coker, 'isn't it, Doctor?'

'Yes,' said Beesdale. 'Anyone who touched anything inside that car, or even poked their head through the window to take a look, has got to be vaccinated right away.'

Alf and Bob and the foreman looked through the enormous open doorway of the garage at the grey Esquire. It was now on its wheels, but clods of turf still clung to the edges of the wings, and deep grazes in the cellulose ran right along one side of the body. The three men gazed at the car with awe; it had lost its innocence.

Bob spoke. He was a knotty, square-bodied man with a rolled

93

cigarette in his mouth that had been out for some minutes.

'Then you better do us both. Alf sat inside, but prob'ly I took a gander myself before we righted her. You never remember these things, do you?'

Mr. Coker said: 'Well, if we want to be on the safe side, this is what we do. We vaccinate you, your friend Alf, and all the people you've been in contact with since you fetched that car in. That means your families, and everyone here at the garage. Then we keep the lot of you under observation for a fortnight.'

They turned their heads to watch him and their awe increased.

'Love a duck!' said Alf.

'It don't mean bein' stood off?' Bob asked Mr. Coker.

'No. You can keep on working.'

'Well, that's all right. I'd go crackers, bein' stood off.'

'He only says that because *I'm* here,' said the foreman, and Dr. Beesdale was kind enough to laugh.

'If you'll get the rest of the staff together,' he said, 'we'll start work here, and then go and visit the families. If any of them are on the telephone we'd like to tip them off and ask them not to go out shopping or answer the door to anyone until they've been disinfected.'

Bob frowned at him. 'Disinfected *too*?'

'Of course. Smallpox can be carried through what we call droplet infection. You can't be too careful.'

'Alf,' said the foreman, as a car drew up at the pumps. Alf was half-way to the doors with his greasy rag when Mr. Coker called out to him.

'Hold it, please.' He turned to the foreman. 'You'll be shut for a few hours, for disinfection. We're sending a van up.'

Alf came slowly back. 'Can't we serve anyone, then?'

'Not anyone. Isn't that right, Doctor?'

'Yes,' said Beesdale, and told the St. John's man to go out and explain things to the customer. 'If you've got a big notice, put it up outside. You're shut until middle day.'

The sunshine was flooding over their feet as they stood at the edge of shadow made by the doorway. In the warmth and stillness of the morning it was hard for them to believe all this. That car out there . . . Everyone would have to be done – and what would Gladys say? She wouldn't believe it at all. Glad never believed anything.

The St. John's man came back. The customer had driven off. Dust settled in the sunshine along the row of pumps.

The foreman said to Beesdale: 'Who was driving the thing when it crashed last night, Doctor? It wasn't anyone from the Crossings, where it belongs – I know that much because they've been through on the phone.'

'The driver's missin',' said Bob, 'isn't he?'

Beesdale swung his bag. 'I believe so.'

'Then who was it?'

'A primary contact of smallpox, so the sooner we start protecting you people the better.' He look at the foreman. 'I should think your office would be the best place, wouldn't it?'

The hall was loud with yapping. Dr. Tewson had begun pitching his voice above the noise when he had realised that nothing was going to be done to stop it. The situation was very serious, he told the lady in the violet dress, and there was much to be done. Her daughter stood behind her to one side, staring at the doctor and the other people defensively. Perhaps it was the noise of the dogs that had set her face in its permanent flinch.

'We have to accommodate you in a new house, while this one is disinfected.' He looked into the blank colourless eyes of the woman. How much did she understand? 'It's inconvenient, of course, but we'll do all we can to help.'

The girl had drawn closer to her mother.

'A new house?' she said. She looked at him as if he were mad. He might have said, a new world.

He talked above the barking, repeating himself, impressing upon them the seriousness of their situation. The man who had been taken to hospital was already in an advanced stage of semi-confluent smallpox, and his life was in danger. Unless they agreed to this emergency step, their lives would also be in danger.

He talked of their new 'decant' house, where there would be new furniture and a radio and all other things. He described how this hotel would be disinfected, so that it would be safe for them to move back very soon – a matter of days.

He talked of vaccination, how painless it was. As he talked, he wondered what kind of thing patience was in a man's mind, that it could carry him along through days and nights of advising and explaining while they watched with frightened and suspicious eyes, shrinking within themselves as they were slowly overwhelmed with this dreadful flooding inwards of alarm that came sweeping across their cups of fragrant afternoon tea and the sound of the mower on the lawn, and Mrs. Joliffe coming this evening for cards. If only Uncle Jack were here! He would never have let this happen.

The big colourless eyes stared out from the barking shadows. '. . . the little ones?'

'Yes, they can be vaccinated.'

He looked down at the dogs. Surely they were immunised against any new germ already. They smelt of their years, neglected by devotion. They barked up at his face.

The girl was saying something and an old man they had called William was standing quite still in a doorway, his arm cupping

95

a piece of newspaper in which were seedlings at all angles in a clod of earth. He held a trowel whose blade was worn bright at the tip and it caught the light from the coloured panes over the hall door.

'. . . not ready for anything like this.'

He said that everything would be taken care of.

One of the men had moved his foot against a dog and the dog yelped and scuttered against the wall near William's feet and the woman ran to the man with her white hands fluttering angrily at his face.

'He tried to bite me!'

'All right, Thompson——'

'Oh how wicked you are – how *wicked*!'

The sun shone through the coloured glass and brought strange hues across their faces.

Some of the earth fell from the newspaper as William bent to pat the dog's head. Tewson saw that tears were coming from the old man's eyes but could not know whether it was pity for the dog or fright that his world in this half-lit place was to be turned upside down. The earth pattered softly on to the floor and he went on his knees, trying to scoop it back into the paper with his trowel while the tall woman harangued the man who had dared to move his foot against the little one.

The barking had stopped, the stridency of the woman's voice replacing it. They stood quivering. The old man scooped with his trowel and for an instant a tear gleamed, falling against the dark of his green apron.

'. . . help with your packing, of course——'

'We need no help. No help.' She stood stiffly, turning on him. The girl was kneeling with two of the dogs bunched in her arms; she kissed their matted fur, devoted in her brown shapeless coat.

She was murmuring, 'It's all right . . . all right. We're all together . . . you can see we're still all together . . .'

Tewson looked down at her.

'It's a difficult time, but we'll help all we can.'

She stared up at him with narrow eyes, drawing back, sheltering the dogs and herself with her brown coat. 'You'll hurt them, when you do it.' Her eyes stared up at the man of whom she had been born afraid, knowing that one day he would come to hurt her dogs.

'Oh no, we don't hurt them.'

'We'd rather we all died than you should hurt them.'

He turned away from her, knowing it was true. These few animals were all this stunted heart had room for. These, and the mother who had withered it.

'Mr. Thompson, shall we make a start?'

'I'm ready Doctor. If we could just use the phone again——?'

She looked at them with the hues of the glass across her face, blue, green, yellow, red and enraged. 'We need no help. We need no help of yours.'

The old man straightened up and the dogs ran to sniff at the scattering of earth, worrying it for scent.

'They won't hurt you,' murmured the girl, and laid her cheek against their heads in turn, tenderly.

Julie had gone to the window and looked out at the sunshine before a nurse sent her back to bed. After the long days of rain the grass ran burning emerald down the verges of the East Road. The sun's heat shimmered above the roadway in the distance and brought the heady scent of the big nettle-bed into the air; it had opened a tulip that she could see from the window.

She had gone back to bed for the sake of the nurse, but could not stay there and was out again now, sitting on the edge with her small white feet dangling from their pyjama-legs. She looked down at them, stretching them until her toes just touched the cold linoleum and then drawing them back with a thrill of pretended danger. Since last evening she had begun to feel the health coming back into her body: health, an abstract word for the perfect juxtaposition and interrelation of a million cells, glands, nerves forming their predetermined pattern of exact accord: but health looked like a blue sky and smelt like a nettle-bed and had the feel of cool velvet.

She began to cry quietly, sitting on the edge of the bed with her feet together, the tears falling with the ease of spring rain, without effort or agony, the spilling over of the job of being alive.

The trolley had gone down to the gates again last night, but not for her. Patients had complained about the noise it always made, although it had rubber tyres. It sent up a tumbril rumbling that filled the night and the heart with fear. It was said that a man in the other wing of the building had died of alastrim, his fever burning him away because he had lain in the dark and had heard the trolley go down three times to the gates, and convinced himself that the fourth time would be for him.

Julie didn't believe the story. It was typical of the rumours that sprang from boredom and isolation. But, lying at night when the clock means nothing and dawn seems unattainable, it was hard not to believe these stories, and become part of them.

A tear fell on to her bare foot and made her laugh, and she looked at the door in case someone should have heard; convention held that one could cry alone, but laughter was a public thing. The teardrop was drying on her foot and beginning to itch. She scratched it, enjoying herself, looking round the room and seeing familiar things with fresh eyes. Every shape looked sane and orderly; a person could never have died among these everyday patterns, for they were permanent and had been since childhood – window-sills especially, for they were the frontier between the known world and the great outside.

Clifford came in and found her kneeling on the bed with her arms stretched out sideways and her head thrown back with her eyes shut.

'What are you doing?'

She looked across at him.

'Flying.'

He came over to her, his pale eyes worried. She had often thought his eyes looked beautiful, calm and clear behind the lenses of his spectacles. He always seemed helpless when he took them off.

'Don't you ever fly, Clifford?'

He studied her chart. 'Not often.'

She felt childish, and got back under the bedclothes, saying humbly: 'It's only because I'm feeling all right again, and not going to die.'

He sat on the foot of the bed, his shoulders in a slump.

'What have you been crying for?'

'Dear life.'

He nodded. She was a normal convalescent. 'You'll be going home soon.'

'I was crying for that, too. Did you know Steven's coming to see me this morning?'

'Is he?' His hands were dug into the pockets of his white coat, making it shapeless. She watched the set of his head and shoulders, sorry for him and unable to communicate her mood. Being very happy was like being tipsy: unless the others were tipsy too you were just a bore. Sadness was more infectious and so was fear.

'Are you worried, Clifford?'

'No.' He got off the bed and went to the window, but she knew the sunshine looked different to him.

'Hasn't she telephoned yet?'

'Does it matter?'

'She knows how busy you are.'

'Yes.'

What did the nettle-bed smell like to him? A nettle-bed.

'I think she was so right to stay up in London when she heard, Clifford. There was nothing she could do here. I got in Steven's way, in the house, even though we only saw each other for a few minutes a day – that's why I came up here to report for duty. A fat lot of use, I've been to you, but the idea was good. Ruth had more sense from the start. If she——'

'It doesn't matter that she hasn't phoned me.'

He turned round but she couldn't see his face clearly because he was standing against the bright window; its expression was in his voice. He was holding himself in, and it was an effort. Julie was familiar with this moment although it had only just come. She and Steven had long ago expected it. 'One fine day,' she had told Steven, 'poor Clifford's going to knock on our door and ask for help.' Steven had said: 'How can we help him? He'll have to rope God in.'

She looked at Clifford's silhouette. 'What does matter, then?'

For a long time he said nothing and his silence and dark outline were just an anonymous presence in the small room, and it seemed to her that Clifford Preston had gone away and left the mere shape of suffering in his place, a phantom *locum tenens*.

'She's not faithful.' And Clifford was back, human and shocked and afraid.

The vastness of his misery made her feel weak. She wasn't well enough to share it.

'I see,' she said, so calmly that he asked——

'You knew?'

She wished she could see him more clearly; it was like talking to someone in the dark, to a faceless voice. The eyes were such an important part of speech.

'You knew?' he asked again, insistently.

'I've never thought about it Clifford.' He didn't know when people were lying because he had never lied himself. It would be as difficult for him to describe the taste of something he had never eaten.

'It doesn't shock you,' he said.

'Infidelity? You're forgetting I'm an infidel.'

'You think you haven't a god, but you must have faith in people at least.' He took a step towards the bed and his dark shape grew against the window. 'You don't uphold adultery. I've heard you say so, in different words.'

She crossed her arms and clasped her shoulders, looking up at him and feeling cold, weak, inadequate. This man could call the strength and the wrath of the Lord on his side, and the sweetness of saints. How could she do anything for him?

'You wouldn't condone infidelity in Steven.' He was at the foot of her bed looking down at her with faint reflected light from the wall striking across his glasses, so that she could not see his eyes. There was no evil in poor Clifford, yet now he seemed malevolent, watching her, standing so still, insisting that she answered him.

'You've been cooped up in this hospital for too long,' she said. 'Fifteen days and nights. It's enough to give anyone emotional claustrophobia. Just because Ruth is free and away from you in London, it makes you think she'd doing things behind your back, and——'

'It's not that.' He lowered his head, putting his hands on the bed-rail, and she was soft with pity for him because he was a good doctor and these hands knew the shape of these bed-rails; he must have leaned on them so many times, talking to the sick and helping them, giving them all he could spare of his strength and sympathy Now he held on to the cold hard rail, lost and beyond her help. Quietly he was saying, 'I know it's true, about her. I suspected it because she'd said something she didn't mean to, and a long time afterwards, when I couldn't bear with it any more, I asked the man.'

'That was brave of you.'

'No. He's not a bad man, you see.'

He raised his head again to look at her. She asked him:

'And he said it was true?'

'Yes.'

'That was brave of him.'

'Or he may not care.' But there was disbelief in his voice, that a man might not care. His hands came away from the rail and he stood up straight, suddenly inspired with his own conviction. 'People *should* care. They *must* care!'

She didn't feel strong enough to cope with him. His dreadful silence, facing her across the little distance; and then his swift crumpling submission; and now his reserve of strength that had straightened his whole body so that he filled the window behind him: she felt small in his presence. Her head had begun to throb and her eyes were stinging as she was made to stare up at him against the light. He was enormous and she could no longer see the sun beyond his great dark figure. She turned in the bed to look for her glass of water. He did not move to help her with it. He was engrossed in his disaster.

He did not move even when a nurse came into the room, but slowly turned his head when she said that Dr. Monks was here to see his wife, so that Steven found him standing at the foot of Julie's bed staring at him as if he were a stranger. The glass of water slipped from her hand as she slumped back in her relief, and the nurse ran forward to help.

NINE

'But he must have known he was upsetting you.'

'He wasn't, really.'

The water had made a dark patch on the bedspread, and the broken glass had scratched the surface of the lino when the nurse had swept it up.

'He must be out of his mind,' said Steven. Anger was still in his eyes.

'Yes, I think he is.' She twisted on to her side because her back and legs were aching. The bedclothes smelt stale and she longed for clean sheets and to be home again.

'There's no reason to upset *you* because his wife's unfaithful to him. You're not responsible and you're not well.' He had thought – had been certain – that Preston had told her. When he had come into the room she had been so white, near tears; and Preston had looked at him as if he were a stranger. He had been ready to face a bitter scene that would have changed his life with Julie; but Preston had left the room without a word.

'I'll talk to him before I go,' Steven said.

'Don't be unkind to him——'

'He can keep his problems to himself while you're trying to get better. Or exercise them on me, or someone else. The priest is the man he should talk to – MacGuire.' He heard the tremor in his voice; he was still angry and frightened. He wouldn't funk the consequences of what he had done, but he had opened the door and believed that he was suddenly face to face with the climax, and unprepared.

Preston mustn't be allowed to run amok in the name of righteousness and charity, dodging out from the shelter of his priest and dodging back like one of the man woman's dogs. Julie must not be hurt.

'Did you know,' she asked him, 'about Ruth?'

He would not look away from her face. 'Yes.'

It seemed so long since he had seen her face with its grey eyes and soft white smile. In these days of the plague so many things happened between one moment, one place, and the next.

'I guessed it, too,' she said.

How confident she was. . . . She believed they were both outside the world of Clifford and Ruth and their misery. She thought they could talk about it here together and alone in this small room and presume privacy.

He hadn't imagined he would feel like this, as if there were a rash on him.

'Did you?' he said.

It would be a relief to tell her. MacGuire was right about that. But when the barrier came breaking down it would smash a part of her and leave its mark. She mustn't ever know.

He was at the edge of tragedy. A word more would carry them over. Clifford had told her, she said, that he had asked the man. The man had admitted it. The words burned in him to be said, deliberatedly, so that the great fear of their being said by accident should be over, the deed finished. I am the man. I was the man with Ruth.

Her eyes would narrow in pain and her white face crumple and she would draw her body back deeper into the bed away from him, and he would not be able to reach out a hand to help because he would be the enemy who had struck at her; and worst of all, there would be no way to tell her that although he had been with Ruth it was Julie he loved and wanted to spend all his life with. She wouldn't believe it. She would believe that, because he had gone to bed with another woman, he loved that other woman and thought more of her and would soon want to go to her and belong to her and possess her. She was incapable of understanding that a man could lust for a prostitute on his late road home and take her and pay her and forget her before he reached his doorstep, having cast no reflection on his wife's attraction, having indulged in no manner of spite or petty vengeance, having followed nothing but his biological impulse to mate with a strange female of the species since he was equipped to serve a thousand and justify his years on earth by the generous procreation of his kind.

Love wasn't a black-or-white affair. He had told MacGuire he didn't love his wife, even now; but already he knew he was wrong.

'Does he think she's playing fast and loose in London?'

'I expect so.' He got up from the bed. He hadn't come here to talk about Ruth.

'Poor Clifford.'

He stood by the window and thought about Preston, wondering if he would be happier or less wretched with Ruth dead than with Ruth a harlot. That would be what he would call her, savouring its sound in morbid fascination, cutting himself to pieces in a frenzy of masochism. But a harlot was a woman who made love for reasons other than love; and no one could say that of Ruth.

'Isn't there anything we can do to help him, Steven?'

He turned and looked at her. 'Not much, but I'm doing what I can.' He had been through a tussle with Buckridge this morning.

They must find the missing woman because she probably had smallpox developing: but she was Mrs. Bradley, a guest at the Crossings Hotel.

'But Dr. Preston might be able to help us find her,' Buckridge had said. His face was an odd colour, his eyes still strained; but he was determined to work his full shift.

'If we can find her without telling him it'll make me very glad. Let's not worry the poor devil while he's up there in that prison. He won't be able to tell us where she is, because he didn't even know she was at the hotel. She's meant to be in London.'

One of the girls came in with some files and Buckridge swung his eyebrows at her and she went out palpitating, closing the door so quietly that Buckridge had to get up and check the handle.

He thought of his own wife, and pretended for a moment that she was at some strange hotel with another man. It was the first time he had wanted to laugh for days, but he stifled the impulse easily enough. With a wife like Maud you could afford to laugh.

'I'm sorry for Preston,' he said.

'Then let's try to help him. He'll be told soon enough that his wife was at that hotel.'

Buckridge watched him as steadily as a bird. 'You're quite sure about this? The other people call her Mrs. Bradley.'

'I'm quite sure. I wouldn't have had to tell you her real name, in confidence, if it weren't important that she's located and dealt with before she can spread her infection.'

He crossed his legs, taking his weight on the left ankle and relieving the injured one. There seemed a cold void in his head and stomach that could only be filled by sleep. He had been awake since the emergency call last night. Nothing was real, of the night, except the lingering smell of her scent that had been in the car and the hideously-furnished room.

'We'll do what we can.' said Buckridge. 'Obviously I'd like to help you keep this quiet for a while, till he's got a chance to sort things out.'

The telephone rang and he passed it to Steven. 'The Crossings Hotel.'

Steven asked the man William if anything had been seen of Mrs. Bradley.

'She's gone.' The voice was too old for these times. The guest had gone in the night. It was in keeping with the strange and sudden businesses of the night that a guest should vanish.

'Nothing has been seen of her since last evening?'

'She's gone, sir.' The old voice scraped in a dry throat and he cleared it, turning away from the telephone to cough and missing part of Steven's question.

'. . . her talking about?'

The receiver was pressed again to the shrivelled dry ear.

'I beg pardon, sir?'

'Can you remember her mentioning any place where she had to go?' The old man's coat brushed against the cord and Steven could hear it along the wires. He had seen William before coming away from the hotel last night, an old man as frightened as the dogs but quieter, already half a ghost in those mad shadows. 'Are you there?'

'Oh yes, sir. But I don't know where she's gone. Madam thinks she's gone a long way. There's victuals gone from the kitchen.'

Buckridge's window buzzed to the vibration of a bus and Steven pressed the receiver more tightly to his head. 'What was that, please?'

'There's food gone from the place. Madam says the lady took it for her journey, perhaps.'

Steven's eye was caught by movement and he looked down through the dirt-film on the window. People were forming a queue at the doors of the new clinic set up in the auctioneering-rooms across the road. He remembered the overturned car. There had been no food inside it but a few spilled chocolates.

He asked the old man about the food and was told it was cheese and some bread, and a bottle of brandy from the cupboard. Was it the only bottle – was there only brandy? Why, no – there was whisky and gin and some of Madam's sloe wine, and two bottles of vintage port.

'But only the brandy is missing.'

'Yes, sir.'

Brandy was Ruth's drink.

'If you have a call from her, or if you hear anthing at all of her whereabouts, will you please be sure to telephone Mr. Buckridge at this office, or telephone me at the number I gave you?'

The old man said that he would be sure; but he thought the lady was gone a long way, with the food and all.

When Steven put the receiver down he realised that Buckridge would not have been listening; he was talking on one of the other telephones. Did he think it odd that Steven should be so certain about this woman? Everyone else called her Mrs. Bradley.

It didn't matter what Buckridge thought. This new contact had to be traced and isolated before she could start a new outbreak – perhaps in London or any large town a long way way from here. The old man thought the lady was gone a long way, with the food and all. But it wasn't in character for Ruth to make a long journey knowing she was a danger to anyone she met. Now that she had lost the use of the car she must hire one or steal one or take a train or a coach. Whatever she did she would expose people to danger: but stealing a car would be the safest way. She had the sense to know that and the courage to do it.

'. . . already told them,' Buckridge was saying into the telephone. 'The dogs can be vaccinated and taken to the "decant" house with them. Don't let them get under your feet. No – the *people*.'

Ruth liked brandy and had taken the food, meaning to go as far as she could in the car before the petrol ran out. But was it for the sake of putting physical distance between herself and the hideous mess or of reaching some definite place where friends might help her?'

A few hours ago she had been on foot, five miles from here in a blinding mist and the dark. She had left blood on the rim of the steering-wheel but her injuries had not stopped her in her determination to escape.

He remembered seeing a wire trap in a spinney years ago: a fleck of blood and a tuft of fur on the cold grey steel, the only sign that anything had been there in the dark alone and was now gone.

'. . . Then use your emergency powers and don't waste your time like a fool.' Buckridge hung up with an angry hand. He said to Steven: 'I've come back in a bad mood. I wonder if it'll matter?'

'At least it'll save you another breakdown. It's the strain of keeping it all inside that gets you in the end. Is there trouble at the hotel?'

'You've been there and seen who runs it. They're just as bad at the cottage where the car turned over. At the last minute the man's wife admitted eating some of the chocolates that she found in the car. At the last minute – just when the team was leaving.' He stared up at Steven. 'Are they ignorant or careless? Don't they *mind* dying like flies?'

Steven gave him a cigarette and limped to the door. 'I hope you don't have to tell anyone, yet.'

'We've got to find this woman. You know that. She's a serious menace all the time she's at large, and if I tell anyone her real name it'll be because it'll help to trace her. It's all I can promise.'

Steven held the door open. 'Will you be sending out an appeal?'

'We've done that. It'll be on the one-o'clock news and in various papers. Mrs. Bradley, a guest at the Crossings Hotel.'

Buckridge was picking up a telephone when Steven left him, going through the main operations room and out into the sharp early-morning street. Looking up at the sky he had closed his eyes to smell the air and think with a longing that was new to him. . . . I shall be seeing Julie today.

'Tell me what's happening in the town,' she asked him.

'Happening?'

'We don't get much news. People haven't the time.'

105

He sat on her bed again, trying to remember what was happening in the town. 'People are frightened.' A woman with a grey face had looked at him with horror slowly tightening across her face until it was a mask and she had seemed to shrink back from him . . . *No* . . . *No* . . . she had said, shrinking away from him as if it were he who had the rash and not her son, the precious boy upstairs, the stricken angel . . . *No* . . . *No* . . . she had said, softly and more softly, shrinking away from him until suddenly she had turned and run up the stairs with the door swinging and Collins clearing his throat. 'They hear about a friend going down with this thing,' Steven told Julie, 'and it starts them worrying. It's different from the way they behaved in the war——'

'Yes. In the clinics——'

'You noticed it?'

'It's because they don't understand what they're up against. There's all this mystery and witch-doctory.'

'You could hear a bomber squadron coming, and duck if you were lucky. This plague needs a different kind of courage, something near Oriental fatalism, and we haven't got it in this country. But it's brought the queues back. There's a new clinic set up in the auction-rooms and another one out at the Tower.'

'I heard there'd been a big rush for vaccine. It's the Royalty outbreak, is it?'

'Yes. It sets them all panicking again but it's not a bad thing. If it goes on long enough the town will have more vaccine in its blood than variola, and that'll be that.'

The silence drew out a little and he put his hand over hers. 'You don't want to talk about that.'

'No.' She had a faint private-looking smile. 'But you came here to talk to me and cheer me up, so you have to turn it all on. I know how difficult it is. I used to see the stranger in the wards on visitors' day, curling themselves up in embarrassment with one eye on the clock – and the relief, the enormous relief when time was up!' She began giggling. 'I saw one man just jab his hat on and run, and we found him lurking about in the nurses' room later because he took the wrong door in his hurry!'

He felt laughter rising in him but was afraid of it and let a little of it come with niggardly caution, as if he were moving a mended limb for the first time and feared it might break again.

'He was still madly in love with her and they'd only been married a year' – and she had to stop and gulp because she was becoming inarticulate as she held on to his hand – 'but he was off like a shot when they told him it was time, and his poor little wife was in tears about it – a post-Cæsar and a bit weepy anyway – and when they told her he'd been dragged out of the nurses' room she was hysterical!'

The laughter felt good in him, a kind of drunkenness rising and

106

taking charge of him while he held Julie's hand and felt it trembling to her subsiding giggles as with her other hand she fumbled for a handkerchief-tissue and wiped her eyes.

'So if they find you in the nurses' room in a few minutes, darling, I shan't cut up rough. . . .'

Before he left her he said: 'Buckridge is back, looking like death and with a bad temper. He sent his good wishes to you.'

'Please give him mine. And how's the Army doing?' She had taken a liking to the young captain in charge of the disinfector team behind St. Martin's.

'Working day and night. People stand round and watch it, because all the cinemas are closed and a solitary diet of television's getting on their nerves. What was that young chap's name?'

'Captain Elliott.'

'I'll give him your regards when I see him, shall I?'

'Please.' The laughing had left her weak but it had eased them both. 'You'll have to go now, darling. Thank you for coming. I know what a bore it can be, in the middle of——'

'It was all I could think about, Julie.'

He came back to her bed and looked down at her. The tension in his voice had surprised her. He said: 'I'll never forget that poor devil saying to me: "She's got alastrim." I think I asked him if he was lying, and he said I could see the reports of the test for myself. He was having his supper. Some bread and cheese, sitting there alone.'

With the deserted dining-hall full of echoes and the one high light burning like a candle in a cathedral. He had been sitting there alone with his bread and wine, quiet with misery, cold with the shock of her immeasurable sin and nearly sure that the man was Steven, who came and found him alone in the great bleak hall, and said: 'You live well, here.'

One had no means of knowing that sometimes a thing one says to a person is unthinkable, at a given moment. One can only look back in horror.

Clifford had asked him to join him with a glass of wine. That had been his answer. 'Try a glass.'

The scene came back to him because he had never thought about it until now, when all its colours were complete. Its few words had meaning now and he could remember most of them. 'It's alastrim. Congratulations.' Said with no irony, no bitterness. 'You're lucky,' he had said, and he had wished aloud to Steven that Ruth would have a child, feeling but not explaining to Steven that it might be the answer, might rouse her maternal instinct and satisfy the needs in her that he somehow failed to, even though he could give her a child, her need of a love that was not his. And all the time he had talked, he had been nearly sure. . . .

'What is it, darling?' She stared up at him.

'I was thinking about Clifford.'

Sitting beside him on the bench, sharing his food and bearing him no enmity. This was what these people meant by 'love', so far removed from moonlight and roses.

The echoes had gone worrying upwards into the shadows of the hall. . . . 'It's time you asked people for help, you know.'

'I always find it difficult. They've got enough worries of their own, especially at a time like this. But you. . . .'

'I've just got my reprieve.'

And then for the first time a trace of bitterness: 'Yes. You've a flair for phrasing things.' And he had wanted at once to hear more about Julie and had made Clifford convince him that it was true, that she wasn't dying. Ruth didn't matter, and they had gone on talking about Julie until the woman had come in to clear their things away . . . and Clifford had said to her that he was sorry they were late. It wasn't until they had left the dining-hall that Steven had asked him about Ruth – and then what was it he had said? He must remember as accurately as he could, because the words had their full meaning only now. He had begun with a kind of apology. . . . 'It doesn't concern me very deeply, but I'd like to get it straight.' And had taken care that his meaning should be clear: 'Have you ever made love to her?'

Even though he must have been nearly sure, there must also have been a hope, the answer to all his solitary prayers that this thing might not have happened, that it was not Steven, nor any man at all. He would know in a moment, know for sure and for ever; but he had thought to put his tormentor at his ease, saying: 'We're civilised people. There won't be a brawl. It's just that I want to know.'

There had been only one untruth. 'It doesn't concern me very deeply.' It was killing him.

Julie said: 'I didn't know you felt sorry for Clifford.'

'It's new.'

She hugged her shoulders, her chin on one hand. 'You used to say he was a drip.'

'That was a long time ago.'

'Not very long.'

'It was before I heard you were going to be all right. All new things began from there.'

She said without looking at him, 'I haven't been very certain you wanted me back. There were things on your mind. When I volunteered as a nurse it wasn't necessarily going to be temporary, until the plague's over. I thought it might be a good idea to keep out of your way——'

'That's——'

'No, please. I thought I'd lost what little understanding I'd ever had of you. You weren't easy to get through to, any more. I pretended to myself that I was the capable little woman who could handle her difficult husband with a light touch and profound understanding. A kind of domesticated Nightingale. But I was miles out, darling, miles out.' She looked up at him. 'You're a very private person, Steven. People think you haven't a heart, just because you don't flash it around like a gold watch.'

Someone had told him this, not long ago. He tried to think. It was MacGuire. MacGuire looking like a needy monk in the disinfection room, piercing him with his black pointed eyes, telling him he daren't show his heart in case people would see it. Were those his words? They were something like that. He could remember MacGuire less easily than Preston. He must ask the priest one day: 'What was it you said about my heart?'

'The only thing is that it makes it a bit difficult,' Julie said, 'for me to get through to you when I must – and there are times when I must, because I love you.'

Her appeal hurt him and he realised that hurt was a new thing, exquisitely painful. She went on talking but he didn't listen because he had to assess these new feelings as he became aware of them, because they seemed tremendously important. Something human was emerging from this monastic shell.

'. . . and working as hard as you are. You should tell me to dry up until you're less busy. But I suppose I'm a bit weepy, like the girl with the Cæsar, and inclined to . . .'

The boys, Bill and Martin – did they think of him as human, as a person they could talk to? A faint memory came, the far sound of Martin's voice beyond the window where the roof of the conservatory ran down in a bright cascade of glass to the dark green rhododendrons, the curtain moving to a breath of wind that crossed the garden and carried the small boy's voice – 'It's no earthly good asking Daddy. He'll say he can't think about it now because he's working.'

Julie didn't know he wasn't listening, because she was not looking at him but talking into her folded arms. 'And I shouldn't have left you alone in the house to cope with it all singlehanded. They'd have had to cart me up here in any case because I was ill – but I *decided* to leave you in the lurch, and that was an awful thing to do. It was cowardly. I should have *asked* you if I was getting in your way. . . .'

It had been no good asking Daddy. You couldn't ask him if you could build a Dinkie-Toy track behind the summerhouse, and you couldn't ask him if you were getting in his way. Then how could they ever have loved him?

Julie had said: 'I told them their father had the entire situation under control,' and he had shouted at her: 'What did you tell them that for?' Not to make his conscience smart, to make him realise the enormity of wanting a holiday when he was needed here. It had been said for the sake of the boys. Failing an object of love there must be an object of pride.

'. . . So I've been lying here, cross with myself, hoping you'll forgive me.'

He stared down at her. Her hair had lost its shine because she had been ill, and the bedclothes were crumpled round her.

His voice was shaking. 'Forgive you?' She looked up, her pupils focusing against the light. 'Forgive *you*?'

'What's the matter, Steven?'

He wanted to touch her dull hair but was afraid to. '*I* am to forgive *you*?'

Not understanding what he was saying she tried to read his eyes but all she could see was that they looked tired and strained. When he could, he said more steadily:

'I want you back.' They were the only words he could think of, and pathetically inadequate. 'I'll try to have the place cleaned up if there's time. Mrs. Chalmers never waters anything, but I've looked after your pink cyclamen and it's going strong.' He tried to think of what else to say, how better to put it; but she was crying into her arms and her hair fell loosely over them.

With her throat full she managed to say, 'I told you I'm a bit weepy, because of being ill.'

He dared to put his hand down and for a moment touched her hair. 'Then you'll feel better if I go.'

She touched his hand without lifting her head. 'Yes. You've got such a lot to do.'

She was hunched in the bed when he went out. Sister Gill was going into Wingfield, but stopped when she saw him. He asked her if she knew where he could find Dr. Preston.

'He's along in Men's Isolation, Doctor.' She asked about Mrs. Monks and he said that she was much better.

'The house must be very empty, without her.'

'Yes.'

She went through the swing doors and he walked on along the passage to the stairs. In Men's Isolation he was told that Dr. Preston was in Number Three. He went in without knocking, opening the door very quietly in case Preston was in the middle of an examination.

The thin curtains were drawn and it was a moment before his eyes accommodated in the half-light. Preston was talking to a nurse; their voices were quiet and they were looking down at Bradley, the case who had been brought in last night from the hotel along the London Road. He was murmuring in his delirium and the sweat was bright across his brow.

Steven watched them for a little time until they sensed he was in the room, and turned their heads.

TEN

'Am I disturbing you?' His voice was no louder than a whisper in the darkened room.

Preston gave a slight shake of his head and went on instructing the nurse. Steven looked at the chart on the wall. This morning's temperature was 105. He looked down at Bradley. The onset of the symptoms had been rapid since last night. He was absorbing his own poisons now and the vesicles were maturating, so that his face was not easy to recognise. These faces all looked the same at this stage, hours before dying: like the face in *The Picture of Dorian Gray*, a hideous record of dissipation and unmentionable sin. Yet they were ordinary decent people with a few faults to balance their virtues. They should never have to look like this.

The black hair was youthful but the features were of no age. A mask resembling Bradley's face but crudely made and with livid colouring would look like this, just recognisable.

He was one of Ruth's lovers.

Unless he had talked in his delirium, Clifford would not know. If he knew, would the sight of this face console him with the salve of vengeance?

He turned away and for a moment watched Clifford's face. His head was bent as he talked quietly to the nurse; in the soft light his face looked younger than ever, the spectacles more earnest. There was no vengeance in him; the word was not in his language.

He looked back at the face in the bed. The poor mouth was moving all the time, but only occasionally did the murmur become fully audible and there was no clear word uttered. Above its intermittent sound Preston went on speaking to the nurse, intoning his instructions with the gentle solemnity of a prayer. Steven listened with a mounting revulsion of himself. What Bradley had done, he had done. In Preston's eyes their sin was as monstrous as the aspect of Bradley's face. In his eyes, Steven wore this face, the countenance of grievous sin. And to a man like Preston there could be only pity for a face like this. That was why he had thought to put his tormentor at his ease while he had waited for the admission that would confirm his misery.

A word came from Bradley's distorted mouth. It sounded like 'care'. One clear word had risen from the tumbling spate of thoughts that were running their feverish way through his mind.

Someone must take care. Or he didn't care. Or no one seemed to care. The context, already whirling away behind the onrush of new thoughts, might have been anything. He was with someone, talking to them, someone perhaps out of his childhood and dead by now, someone he loved or hated or just had to talk to. They were there in the sick intimacy of his dying mind and their image had its shape in his delirium as he talked to them – his mother, or an enemy, or Ruth.

If he regained consciousness before death came, this world of white uniforms and drawn curtains and the great bright rod of the thermometer would be less real than the other where he was talking to someone now, his mind whirling and twisting headlong through the nightmare memories as if he must live through all his life again while these few hours were left.

'. . . *Soon.* . . .'

Another word rising like a bubble from the dark flying current; a meaningless word; a Chinese word. The mouth had uttered it from habit; the mind that had inspired it wasn't aware of this unreal half-lighted and white-uniformed world where people might be listening. He had a world of his own and was locked in with its faces, voices, hands and the remembered regard of eyes as they listened to all he had still to tell them, while his body lay at the mercy of the virus that multiplied and multiplied according to the law of its own survival, by which same law this larger organism was condemned to incidental death.

His hair was black. Her lover would never grow old.

When Steven looked up from the bed he saw that someone else had come into the room, one of the sisters of the isolation block. She said quietly to Preston: 'Somebody telephoned half an hour ago, Doctor, to ask about him. She wouldn't give her name.'

He said to the nurse: 'If he regains consciousness, tell him, please. Meanwhile spray the nose, mouth and throat and keep up the compresses.'

Steven moved away from the bed. What had the woman's voice been like on the telephone? Young, arrogant, vibrating from the strong slender throat where the barbaric ivory necklace glowed white and shivered as she moved. . . . How is Mr. Bradley please? My name doesn't matter.

There might be other women who would telephone to ask about him and not wish to give their name; but he was as sure of her presence in this room, brought alive here by the tenuous threads of the telephone wires and the sister's message, as if her scent were suddenly in the air. Some kind of sympathy, an electro-biological transfluence outside the known senses of perception between animals, linked him with this woman he had no love for but whom he understood and of whom he was aware with a

112

certainty that sometimes frightened him.

Ruth had telephoned.

She mustn't use telephones or touch people. A few hours ago she had been in the same room as Bradley, perhaps trying to nurse him. She had been exposed to gross contamination. She was now a carrier. Wherever she went she was a menace to human life.

But she knew this. She was a doctor's wife. Was she out of her mind, then?

'. . . And ask Father MacGuire, Doctor?'

Preston was turning away to the door.

Ruth would never endanger people willingly. There was no selfishness in her, or cowardice. He didn't understand how she could have decided to use a telephone and leave the virus on the mouthpiece and along the soft absorbent covering of the flex.

He heard Preston saying: 'I understand he refused to see Father MacGuire, but if he regains consciousness you could ask him to come here.'

He opened the door and Steven followed him out into the glare of the sunlit passage.

'I hope I didn't upset your wife, Steven.'

His voice was strong and steady and Steven realised for the first time that Clifford had changed in these last few weeks. There was no nervous hesitancy, no awkwardness, no reliance on the phrase that had been a habit with him for so long – 'as a matter of fact'. He walked the same, pigeon-toed, his body sloping forward to catch up with the thoughts that were going ahead of him; he stood in the same way, his narrow head down an inch, listening, preoccupied; but he had changed.

'Yes, a little.'

'I'm sorry.'

'Julie's worried because she couldn't help you. She's not very strong yet and can't think out big problems——'

'It was stupid of me. It should have occurred to me that——'

'You're fagged out, Clifford. We all are. She's all right now.'

They moved along the passage slowly, their shadows floating along the wall. The sun's warmth brought the smell of floor-polish to the air. 'That man's going to die, soon.'

Preston nodded and asked: 'You sent him in, didn't you?'

'Yes.'

'They say his wife's missing. Is that right?'

'Yes.'

'She'll be a danger.'

'They're doing all they can to trace her. Clifford——' and he knew what it was to hesitate – 'when I found you with Julie I thought she looked upset because you'd told her. MacGuire's been talking to me.'

'No, I haven't told her. Father MacGuire says you'll want to do it yourself.'

Their shoes squeaked on the polished floor and in the narrow passage each was aware of the intimacy of the other's presence Once as they walked slowly along their shoulders touched and Steven moved away, feeling that even so light a touch would bruise the man beside him.

'Give me a little time to think about it. I have the right.'

'Every right.' Preston stopped outside the door of a cloakroom and Steven expected him to take off his glasses and wipe them; but he did not.

'Have you heard from Ruth?' He put the question quickly, to get it said.

Preston studied him for a second and then said: 'No. Why?'

'I'd like to think she phoned.' There must be some way of asking where she was meant to be staying. She might have gone back there, taking the disease into London. Clifford watched him, looking a little surprised by his careless arrogance in asking about Ruth. 'Is she still in London?' Steven persisted.

'As far as I know.'

There seemed no way of getting it out of him without telling him that she had been living with Bradley at the Crossings Hotel and was probably now infected. Surely he would lose his reason if he were told that.

'If she rings up,' Clifford said, 'I'll tell her you were kind enough to ask after her.'

In any other man Steven would have been certain it was bitter sarcasm.

'Thank you.' He turned away and heard Clifford going into the cloakroom as he walked down the passage to the stairhead.

Sister Catteridge stopped him on the stairs to ask if he were going into the town. He said he was.

'There's some mail for the post.' Her smile was a faded apology. 'I wondered——'

'Of course, Sister.'

'I'll have them left in the disinfection rooms for you. It's very kind of you, Doctor Monks.'

He reached the ground floor and passing through the hall block he thought to look in at the switchboard room.

'There was a call from a woman, about ten or fifteen minutes ago. She was put through to Sister Barnes in Men's Isolation. She wouldn't leave her name.'

The girl said she would check it for him.

He stood looking through the big glass doors.

Ruth had phoned to ask about Bradley but not to speak to Clifford. She had not gone home to their flat in the Grove, because Steven had called there this morning with a note for her and had dropped it into the letter-box. It just said that if she needed help she should phone him or get a message to him: but surely if she needed help she would ask for an ambulance to pick her up.

He felt there was a point he was missing.

'... Doctor?'

He turned. 'Yes?'

'It must have come from a call-box. It wasn't a private subscriber.'

'A call-box – where? London?'

'Oh no. Local. Somewhere in Kingsbourne.'

He nodded. 'Thank you.'

On the way to the disinfection rooms he tried to answer the new questions. Ruth had taken food from the Crossings Hotel, perhaps planning a long trip. But she was still in the town. Because she was now without the use of a car? But she had been driving towards the town when she crashed.

If she had taken the food so that she could keep away from people and not infect them, why had she used a telephone-box?

He did not understand her any more. But she must be traced. He would see Buckridge, because only he and Buckridge knew who Mrs. Bradley was.

Stopping by the pillar-box he took the disinfected bag and opened it, tipping the letters into the slot without touching them. They scuttered into the wire basket.

The bright sunshine hurt his eyes, though the shower in the disinfection rooms had refreshed him. He had stood shivering under the cascade of cold water that roared past his ears and ran down over his closed eyelids and mouth, pattering on to the tiles at his feet. For a few minutes he had lost his identity and was just a naked man with his thoughts locked in the dark of his head that was sightless and deafened by the water and shrunk by its chill.

The sun flashed on the chromium of cars and the windows of shops. The pavements looked deserted, as they did every day now, but the usual group of people stood at the fence watching the troops at work in the playground behind St. Martin's. The throb and rattle of the disinfection plant sent echoes from the big wall of the school.

There was no time to see Captain Elliott and give him Julie's message. He was warmed by the thought of her, and knew he had not said anything he had meant to say in those few minutes with her, except that he wanted her to come back.

At the doors of the auction rooms in Market Square there stood the tail-end of a queue for vaccination. The few people looked patient, standing in their dull-coloured clothes, some of them with packets of sandwiches. In the early days there had been emotion: excitement, panic, humour, ignorant anger against the authorities for letting this thing happen in their town. Now there was apathy and the undercurrent of fear that crept into the houses and out of them with the teams from the Health Department calling and leaving. The shops were quiet, the cinemas and dance-halls closed. People in buses sat with arms narrowed at their sides because the people next to them were not safe, not to be trusted. The law of the untouchable was in the town. You never knew. It was best to stay indoors.

Steven backed his car among the others outside the Town Hall and the queue turned its few quiet faces to watch him go into the building.

He asked for Dr. Tewson, but he was still on the London road job; Beesdale had come back, but was down at the new clinic at the Tower; but Buckridge was in his office, sitting at his desk as if he had never moved since Steven had seen him last. The top of his gold pen winked at his breast-pocket, catching the light of a sunbeam that glowed through the dirty window.

'How is your wife?' he said.

'Much better, thank you.' He was touched by Buckridge's thought when there was so much else on his mind. 'She's delighted to hear you're back at work. How do you feel?'

'I've not time to think.' He slammed a drawer and when one of the telephones rang he switched the call through to the main room. Steven asked:

'Have you traced Mrs. Bradley?'

'No.' He looked up at the clock. 'There'll be a broadcast in an hour, and the first edition of the *Gazette's* due out.'

Steven offered him a cigarette and when they had lit them he said: 'I don't think she's near a radio, and if she were, I doubt if she'd alter her plans.'

Buckridge looked away from him and Steven felt he was embarrassed by this problem.

'What *are* her plans, would you say?' Before Steven could answer he went on – 'You see, I'm not used to this kind of thing, Doc. Up to now I've respected your wishes and not told anyone who "Mrs. Bradley" is. But it makes the work very difficult – don't you see? Why not break it gently to Dr. Preston, clear the air, and go all-out to find her?'

It seemed such a simple solution.

'Aren't you going all-out now?'

'Well, yes. But I – I mean she has friends and relatives. If the appeal were for Mrs. *Preston* to come forward there'd be reactions at once from people who know her. She might even be staying with one of them. To broadcast a message to a non-existent Mrs. Bradley doesn't make sense, unless she hears it herself and realises

116

it means her.' He opened a drawer for no reason and peered down into it, avoiding Steven's eyes. 'I suppose you're certain it *was* Mrs. Preston at the hotel?'

'Yes.' Her scent in the car and the room, and the oval of mauve soap.

Buckridge swung his head up, obviously making an effort to face him. 'Then let's get it over and tell him. I don't see it would do all that much harm. It would be painful for him, of course – we all feel we can trust our wives, and – and sometimes these things just don't work out' – and he peered into the drawer again, so that Steven knew that to talk to him about infidelity was to discuss a snowstorm with a Zulu. It was something he had read books about and seen on the pictures, something he would never begin to understand because his marriage was his entire world and he lived in it.

The cigarette tasted bitter in Steven's mouth. He stubbed it out and said: 'I've just been talking to Dr. Preston. I don't know what it would do to him if we told him. But the main thing is that there's no need to. He doesn't know where his wife is. He thinks she's in London, but——'

'*London?*'

'But she's not. She's somewhere in Kingsbourne.'

'How do you know?' The mention of London had unnerved him.

'She phoned the hospital an hour ago, without giving her name.'

Buckridge faced him because he was thinking hard and there was no room for embarrassment. 'Where was she telephoning from?'

'We don't know. A call-box. If it had been me she was phoning I would have tried to make her see reason, but——'

'What did she tell Preston, then?'

Steven hesitated, realising that Buckridge was Buckridge. If a woman rang up her husband's hospital it could only be to speak to her husband. Night followed day.

'She didn't talk to him.'

'Then——'

Buckridge gave it up and slammed the drawer.

'Listen,' said Steven. 'I know both of them fairly well. If it would help us to find her by telling him she's in this mess, I'd do it myself. But he can't help us if he doesn't know where she is.'

'He'll have to know sooner or later, won't he?'

'Yes. But she might not live long.'

Buckridge stared at the window. 'That's true.' His head swung to look straight at Steven. 'Do you think she's lost her reason? Anyone sensible would ask for help——'

'She's not a person to take the sensible path. She doesn't much like paths of any kind.'

'As you say, you know her well. And you've no idea – no intuition – where she might be?'

Steven turned and looked out of the window to where the crows were wheeling above their nests in the square. 'When she left the Crossings Hotel she took some food with her. At first I thought she was going to drive a long way. She'd heard there were people coming to the hotel from here, and didn't want to be found there by anyone who might know her. She's the wife of a local doctor, don't forget. She took the car on an impulse and drove too fast in the mist. When it crashed she escaped on foot – and took the food with her. Now tell me if my reasoning's wrong. If she'd planned to make a long trip, she wouldn't have taken the food out of the overturned car: because now she'd have to go by train or a coach and would come into contact with people anyway – and would therefore be able to buy her food without increasing the risk very much. Yet she took the food with her, although she was desperate to get out of that car and escape. It was important.' He turned and looked at Buckridge.

'Yes, I'm with you so far.'

'Another thing is that when she crashed she was driving towards Kingsbourne, not away from it. And she's here now, because she phoned the hospital from a local call-box. So my feeling is that she's isolating herself of her own free will, living in the open and keeping away from people until she knows whether she's infected.'

He thought of the country near the Crossings Hotel: heath and gorse land, with spinneys along the Wrex, and willow-clumps. At this precise moment, when Buckridge was sitting at his desk, and those people down there were shuffling into the vaccination clinic, and that one crow was floating down to settle above its nest, and the window buzzed to the vibration of the Number Three that was drumming through the square – where was Ruth?

Alone. He was certain she was alone. The food to keep her alive until she could forage for more and go on living until she would know whether she was going to have a future or was going to die. The brandy for warmth at night and solace while she lay in hiding at the mercy of time in which there'd be nothing to do but think.

'Or she might have taken the car,' he said without preparation, 'to use as a shelter. Bury it among the undergrowth somewhere and sleep in it at night——'

'Then she must be mad.'

'I don't think so. But desperate. Desperation makes us do things. . . .' He left it unfinished. She would prefer that kind of isolation to the tedium and indignity of the hospital, and the questions that would be put to her by the contact team while

118

Clifford was there, listening, loathing the sight of her face and her body and the thought of her sins against him.

She was free and alone in the unknown places, responsible to no one. That was Ruth.

Buckridge got out of his padded chair and Steven listened to the creak of its old mahogany legs. It was the sound of a sudden decision. 'If she's isolating herself,' Buckridge told him, 'and keeping clear of people, then she couldn't have rung up the hospital, could she?'

Steven turned away from the window.

'I've been trying to fit that into the picture, and I can't.'

'Are you sure it was her, on the phone?'

'Yes.' Without any evidence. It was an overwhelming certainty that he refused to doubt, because he knew Ruth, and Ruth had telephoned.

'Her infatuation for this man. . . .' Buckridge hesitated.

'Might have driven her out of her isolation to find out how he was. But I don't believe so.'

'We can't have it both ways——' He went to answer the telephone on his desk and Steven stood by the window flogging his brain again, knowing that if he were wrong about one point he could be wrong about them all.

Buckridge was saying into the telephone: 'Tell him to try the other lead. Charles Howarth. He's got the address.'

Steven could hear the other voice, faint and distorted.

'Not yet,' Buckridge said, and rang off. He said to Steven: 'Is Dr. Tewson back here, do you know?'

'He wasn't when I came.'

'Are you working a list?'

'I've no orders. Is there a new case?'

'No. Bradley was the last. But we'll be sitting on a bomb again until we find – Mrs. Bradley, and check on her contacts.' He came back to the window. 'Why don't you go home and get some sleep? There won't be many chances like this.'

Steven nearly said no; but the thought of sheets and the drawn curtains weakened him like the sudden influence of a drug. 'Shall I?' he asked.

'If we need you, we'll call you.'

'Then I'll go. But it seems odd.'

Buckridge was an older man and for a moment put his hand on Steven's arm. 'It seems odd to work half the night, if you look at it that way. The clocks are all up the pole these days. Go and get some sleep.'

In the doorway Steven said: 'You'll let me know if you get any news of her?'

'If I think it's important.' He came out on to the main landing with Steven. Some people were climbing the staircase and they could hear Dr. Tewson's voice. When he reached the landing he left the other two men to go ahead of him into his office and stopped to say good-morning to Steven and Buckridge.

'Is old Beesdale back yet?'

Buckridge said he had gone to the Tower clinic. 'Have you been on fire recently?' Tewson's face was smudged with smuts and his eyes looked red.

'What?' He wiped his face with a handkerchief. Through the open main doors on the floor below came the peal of an ambulance bell going past the Square. 'We had to deal with one, coming back. No one hurt – it was a telephone-box.'

Buckridge made to turn back into his office. 'I suggested Dr. Monks should go home and sleep, unless you've anything——'

'Where was the telephone-box?' asked Steven. The M.O.H. looked at him.

'Up the London road. Yes, you could go and grab some sleep. You had precious little last night——'

'Did you put the fire out in time?'

Buckridge came towards them again, looking at Steven.

'In time for what? There's not much to burn in a phone-box and it was pretty well gutted when we came past.' He finished wiping his face and put his grimy handkerchief away.

Steven knew that she must have begrudged using even a little of the brandy, to start it with.

ELEVEN

When the matron came in, the superintendent had just put the receiver down. He had been talking to the group secretary of the County Hospital Management Committee for twenty minutes and was already trying to find a cigarette.

'How long have we been in quarantine, Matron?'

'Fifteen days, Doctor.'

'Well we've got another sixteen to go. You might pass that on to the staff in your most tactful manner.' He found his cigarettes, knowing what Matron would do. She would stick a notice on the board.

'There's been an extension?'

'Yes.'

'There had to be, hadn't there?'

'Does that make it more acceptable? I'm glad to hear it. You in your turn might be glad to hear that I've told Group that thirty-one days is a long stretch under these conditions. Three of the nurses who elected to stay on during the crisis have died here, and until two days ago we were receiving more cases than Burford – with less room and fewer facilities. I also mentioned that the whole staff from you downwards deserve all possible praise for the way they've kept things running, so don't have the impression that I gave *them* the impression that we can't deal with the work.'

'Thank you, Doctor, but it's what we're all here for.'

He blew his cigarette-smoke towards the open window, knowing she detested the smell. There was a secret air-hole that he knew about, made by some of the staff in the end store-room; he had discovered it one day when he had been alarmed to see smoke issuing from the middle of a brick wall. When people came into this office it was on business, and no one realised what an extensive view there was to be seen from his windows, nor had he enlightened them.

'For someone who dislikes heroes, Matron, you have an ear for their stock expressions. A camel is for carrying things, but it's a bad thing to break its back.' He knew her eyes were on his ash-tray as he flicked his cigarette over it, but didn't deny in his mind that it looked an unhealthy mess.

'I'll tell the staff, Doctor.'

'About the camel?'

'The extension of quarantine.'

'Good. And we might mention, when the notice is being drafted' – he avoided her eyes – 'that everything is being done to see that the quarantine will be lifted at the end of these thirty-one days, even if the epidemic hasn't been contained by that time.' He found himself using the kind of expression that would appear in the notice.

'Very well, Doctor.' But her tone said there was no need to mollycoddle them.

'How is Mary?'

Everyone called the girl Mary. She had come in ten days ago and her life had been saved.

'I've asked Father MacGuire to do what he can with her. I think he's making some progress.'

'Have you seen her today?'

'First thing. I'll be round again this afternoon.'

He touched some letters on the desk. 'These are from her people, and they've telephoned twice today. I'd like to be able to tell them something definite.'

'I'll report to you as soon as I've seen her, Doctor.'

'I'd be glad. But don't hurry Father MacGuire. He might need more time.'

'We've plenty, here.'

He got up from his chair as she left, in keeping with the tradition he had established casually between the two of them as a mark of respect to her. It cut across all the rules of conduct in this jurisprudence place, and for that reason alone would have given him pleasure.

They had put Mary at the end of Roberts Ward when she had left the isolation block. There were screens round her bed, leaving room for a small chair and card-table where she could write; but she had sent only three letters since she had been here convalescing, and those had been to her parents.

The photograph of a young man in Naval officer's uniform was on the window-sill, but the romantic innuendos of the nurses had elicited nothing more than that his name was George. It was an attractive face, and the younger nurses who had daydreams about him thought of him as Roland or Alexander according to choice. They had been ordered not to talk about him to Mary any more, because it was after one of them had told her how lucky she was to know such a wonderful young man that she had cut her wrists.

Father MacGuire said: 'The tulips are out, in the park.'

She sat on the bed in her dressing-gown, and he sat on the flimsy chair. Every time he moved he felt it flexing under him, and tried to keep still.

122

'Are they?' She didn't look up into his bright black eyes, though he often tried to make her, with silences.

'You'll be seeing them in a day or two, Mary.'

'Tulips?' She looked up in a kind of surprise, as if she hadn't realised what he was talking about. He managed to keep her eyes on him for a second or two before she looked down again. It was better than yesterday.

'Tulips,' he said, 'and people.'

'No.'

'With your new hat, Mary.' They had told him she had ordered a new spring hat, with a veil. It was being made for her specially, since she wanted the veil to be heavy and to reach below her chin. They hadn't understood until Matron had explained to them on the telephone.

'It hasn't come yet,' she said.

'It will, before you leave. You're going to promise me, before you leave. You said you would.'

'Everyone isn't like you.'

'Most of them are better.'

'I don't mean – goodness.' She looked at him and to keep her eyes on his he said cheerfully:

'You don't mind a fat old priest seeing your face, but you'd mind it if handsome young men saw it, because they wouldn't look at you as they did before——'

' – It's not that——'

'It is that, child. You're young and used to attracting them and now you think you won't be able to – but that's no reason for trying to do away with yourself, because there's more to this life than flirting.' The chair creaked but he did not notice as he leaned towards her. She was staring at him. 'It's a pity you're going to hide behind a veil. Your eyes are very beautiful and no one will see them.'

For an instant she forgot, and he saw the look she must have given so many young men when they had said nice things to her.

'You can't fool me,' she said.

'Nor can you fool me. I'm not leaving you until you've given me your promise. I think you would keep a promise, to me.'

She whispered, 'I can't go out there. I know I can't. I'm not – not strong enough. It makes me sick to think about it. It always will.' She turned away from him and spoke past her shoulder. 'I'd been thinking about it a lot in the night, that time, and went to the lavatory to be sick, and then I did it.' She moved one wrist and dropped her hand again. The marks were a soft red, still healing.

'That was selfish of you.'

Still she wouldn't cry.

'Everyone's got the right to do that.'

123

'No. You don't only belong to yourself. You belong to all of us, and we need you with us. What a dull place the world would be without you!'

'I hate the world.'

'We don't mind, because we understand. You'll understand, one day soon. Until then, you need us as badly as we need you.' He got up from the chair and moved it back to the wall.

'Don't go,' she said, and looked up in fright.

'I'm not going.'

'Only you understand. No one else does.'

'I'm the only one in the world who knows all about Mary? You'll give me a swollen head, because that's a big compliment. But of course you're wrong – there are lots of people like me, and they'd help you more than I can. They can give you the two things you must have if you mean to go on. Love and refuge.'

'I don't understand.' She moved on the bed, trying to find a different position; but she had used all the positions in these past days and was at the mercy of the trap they had made for her. At night when the others slept she walked down the ward, pretending it was a street of shops. 'My mother and father love me.'

'And they have a refuge for you. But you are their child, and you won't suffer their pity for long. They'll have to watch every word in case you sense a double meaning and they'll find you on the stairs one day, trying to hear what they're saying about you behind the door——'

'I don't care what they'll say——'

'You care too much. Your home would become a trap for you like these screens, and then you'd go into the lavatory again and scratch at your wrists with broken glass to spite them.'

She said, 'You're horrible.' And now she began to cry because it was a relief to hear the truth pattering softly on the desolate thoughts that were lying parched in her mind.

'You don't think about other people,' he said.

'I think about you.'

'Only because I can help you.'

'I don't deserve it.'

'You don't mean that.'

'There's *some* good in me!' She turned her face to look up at him and her eyes were angry. The tears had stained the dreadful pocking of her face and he smiled down at her.

'I was so afraid you'd lost your self-respect,' he said, 'but there it is, shining like gold. It's all we need to work on——'

'I called you horrible.'

'I've called you a lot of things too. It's better than throwing saucepans because we shan't wake people up.' He sat on the foot of the bed, thinking as he watched her that if everyone were born with this red riddling of marks on their face the child who was

124

born with smooth skin would begin a life of tragedy. The world was afraid of a freak and showed no mercy. 'Tomorrow,' he said, 'we'll find out which convent is nearest your home.'

'Convent?' It was as if he had said prison.

'Yes.'

'But I couldn't!'

'They're not cold places, you know. These days there's central heating. We're very up-to-date.'

'But I couldn't be a *nun*!' She was horrified.

He touched her hand to comfort her. 'I don't suggest you take the faith child. Let's not resort to desperate measures.' There was gold in the black of his eyes.

She said quickly – 'I mean, I don't believe in it.'

'That doesn't matter, as long as It believes in you. But I must make this clear to you before you take too much fright. You could go into a convent as a lay person and find your refuge there among people who are too busy to think about your face, but not too busy to help you and love you. When you feel steadier in your mind you can leave the convent and owe it nothing.'

She didn't look up as the swing-doors thumped behind the screens; she was intent upon MacGuire's face.

'I'd have to learn,' she said.

'About God?'

She nodded.

'You've been learning since you were born, and you'll go on; but no one will try to teach you at the convent. We are eager to share what little we know, but we don't want to press it on people like free coupons for soap-flakes. If you want to you can work there – clerical work or cooking, or helping with the garden – you'll want to do something to keep your hands and mind alive. But no one will suggest for a moment that it might help you to pray or read a little from our books. The books and the doors would be always open, and your spirit as free as the air.'

He looked up at Matron, who was standing in the gap made by the screens.

Mary turned her head, one hand flying up in case it was a stranger.

'It's only me, Mary.'

'We rather expect people to knock,' said MacGuire, 'when they call on us, don't we?'

Matron looked down into the fine strong eyes that were as black as her father's had been; there seemed a little triumph in them. 'You've been here long enough, Father MacGuire. You're getting a bad reputation among my staff.'

'Has anyone a good reputation, among your staff?' He stood up with a great show of effort and said to the girl: 'I'm going to let you off making your promise, if you'll think this idea over, because if you think about it you won't do anything spiteful.'

They heard the matron going away down the ward.

'It'd seem like running away from life again.'

'No,' he said. 'Towards it.'

.   .   .   .

The evening sunshine filtered through the smoke of the chimneys of the box-factory that had started work again, and its light rusted the narrow street where Buckridge's car was standing, outside Number 17. He had left the front door open as a gesture, and the air moved in. A cat crept with delicate feet on the doorstep, touching its whiskers along the paintwork, reconjuring the smells that had been here sixteen days ago when the door had last been left open as wide as this.

Inside the front room the clock ticked on the mantelpiece, measuring the silences between the talk. Mrs. Prebble was in one of the armchairs, the younger boy with her and his brother Sidney, the man of the house, leaning against the wall by the television set. Buckridge had the other armchair and was perched forward in it, his sleeve in a sunbeam that came down yellow through the lace curtains. They all watched his bushy grey eyebrows while he drank the tea.

He had been telling them about young Jack, who was being looked after in the nursing-home, and they had listened with the apathy of people who had passed through danger and grief and who didn't want to hear any more.

But his voice was dry and musical, and there were his eyebrows to watch.

'I told him it was best,' he said. 'It was partly his own idea.'

He finished his tea and the smell of soot came back as he looked for somewhere to put his cup.

'Sidney——'

'Yes Mum.' He took the cup from Mr. Buckridge, who sat back and said:

'He thinks you won't want to see him back here for a while, and of course I said he was making a big mistake there, but if he takes a job as a steward with the airline again, or better still in a ship, he'll have a chance to forget all this and see things differently. He's a sensitive boy, as you know.'

'Yes,' said Mrs. Prebble. She hadn't thought much about young Jack in the past few days. He had always been for going off on his own, and she had never really got to know him like the other two.

'When he's ready, we'll fix him up, and when he comes home again it'll be summertime probably. The sun makes all the difference in the world.'

The clock's tick picked at the silence.

'The Welfare people have been to see you?' he asked.

126

'Oh yes. They've been very kind. They've thought of everything.'

He nodded and stood up, shaking his jacket straight. The gold pen-top flickered in the yellow light. 'Of course, you can leave the house now. That's what I came to tell you.'

'Yes.' She stood up too, and Sidney moved away from the wall, tucking his chewing-gum in his cheek and thinking it would be funny without Daph. It was like having a tooth out, right out of the middle of you.

Mr. Buckridge was shaking hands with Mum, not shaking her hand really but just holding it while they looked at each other.

'You're a very wonderful woman,' he said, and the younger boy thought that was a pretty slick way to talk, with Dad only gone a fortnight.

She said, 'It'll stop now, won't it? For us?'

'Yes, it's over now.' He took his hand away from the thin chill of hers.

Sidney came with him to the front doorstep and looked out at the street, where the light was turning to purple against the dark slate roofs.

'Coming out?' asked Mr. Buckridge. He went on to the pavement but the boy shook his head.

'I've got nowhere to go,' he said.

'You've plenty of friends, surely.'

'Them?' He gave a feeble grin. 'All they got to do is put letters in the door, with rhymes on. We've had a lot of 'em. Not that I care, but it give Mum a turn sometimes. He looked at Buckridge with his tufted boy's head on one side. 'Don't they *know*?'

'They know, but they don't trouble to think. Look well after your mother, and if she feels very bad, give me a ring from the phone-box at the end of the road.'

'We'll manage okay, thanks.' He looked out at the row of houses suspiciously, counting his enemies. 'Jack couldn't help it, could he?'

'No more than any of us could. And if anyone doesn't understand that, you'd best push their face in for them.'

'I got better use for me hands.'

. . . .

Police dogs had been sent into a four-mile area surrounding the telephone-box that was burnt out. There had been dew in the early morning, but the scent was nearly twenty hours old. There were two Alsatians, Rexie and Brutus, with a handler for each, and they had dodged about for longer than half an hour before Rexie had gone trailing off to a gate a hundred yards down the London road. He had beckoned his handler with impatient whimpering and then leapt the gate before they could let him through.

Brutus stayed near the box, following the three other scents to the edge of the roadway, where they were lost at the point where Dr. Tewson and his team had climbed back into their car.

The men worked until noon, picking up two different tracks that sometimes crossed. The sun was warm with no wind and the dogs were sweating their tongues out and the handlers thirsting for beer.

'There shouldn't be two of them. We weren't told to find two.'

'One of the farm men, likely.'

'If I'd been one of the farm men we'd be up there now, pulling the dogs off.'

They came back to the road and stood in the shade of the hedge. They had called at the farm, but no one had crossed the fields from there to use the telephone-box; there was a telephone at the farm.

'Whoever used that box came through this gate here and broke the open ground, and they never went up to the farm.'

'They've been every bloody-where else, then.'

A thrush tugged at worms, listening and digging round the tussocks, bold as brass even when the dogs came back and tried to move the men.

'You're daft, the pair of you.'

Brutus sat down and spilled saliva. He wouldn't work when his handler was resting.

'We'd better water them.'

'They been in the river twice.'

'And got rid of it. Come on, you dozy thing.'

The other man followed with Brutus, who loped, bored with it.

The Wrex was still dragging twigs along its banks, but the two days of clear sky had brought the water-mark down and the footbridge was dry again with mud caked on its planks.

The dogs nuzzled the water, their feet sliding and making grooves in the fresh mud. A dragonfly shimmered below the willows and the men sat watching it.

'They have a bust-up, or something, Fred?'

'Eh?'

'She's a married woman, isn't she?'

'I dunno. Is she?'

'Well, they call her *Mrs.* Bradley, don't they?'

'That don't mean she's married, does it?'

The dragonfly went floating among the reeds.

'I s'ppose not.'

Rexie came up the bank and sat down and shut his eyes in the sun to relish the slaking.

'Why couldn't they give us something?'

'She'd took everything with her, and the place has been disinfected, since.'

'Fat hopes.'

'I don't know if you've noticed anything, Fred.' He pulled a blade of grass and sucked at it. 'Rexie's track went across the river twice, but yours never did. It followed the bank from up near the farm to well past here.'

'That's right.'

'You ask me, I'd say Rexie's on to the woman, and the other one was out here looking for her. Looking for her in the river, right along the bank here.'

'Then he got the same luck as us. Brutus, you lop-eared mug.' The dog lifted from his haunches and came to be stroked.

'You'll fill your belly once too often, you will.' He looked at the cool ripples below the bank.

'They had to have water.'

'I don't like this river, though. There's a worse risk than ever, after they're dead. The only way is to burn them. There's not one they haven't cremated.'

A ring spread where a small fish rose.

'There's nothing dead in that river. The dogs would've got on to it.'

.   .   .   .   .

The evening sun that glowed through the smoke of the box-factory washed the walls of King's Hospital with a clear rose light, and the many windows seemed on fire. In the dining-hall the talk had been higher, more excited, and there were jokes already circulating about the official notice that had gone up on the board.

The superintendent was being referred to solemnly as the governor and the sisters and nurses as warders. Those with a little knowledge of prisons made much of it, and there was already a term for the extension of quarantine: the Stretch. The news, bad though it was, broke the boredom for them, and found their humour.

Later as the light turned gold in the windows and then ran red across the west there came another change of mood. It spread from Men's Isolation and hushed the voices along the corridors, lowered the eyes in the wards and staff-rooms, closing a door more quietly in the big main hall and muting footsteps on the stairs. It always happened in this way; it was the ill wind that brought no one any good.

The lights were switched on and the building lost touch with the outside and the dark, becoming like a ship far from land, all its life its own and the world forgotten for the night.

Fevers were worse at night, and the spirit was low. For a few the day had been a battle and they had won, and were still here; but now there was fear of tomorrow.

This evening the nurses were not helpful; they said very little and there was nothing behind the smile as they went about more quickly as though it were important to show that nothing had happened. But trays went down with things untouched and books were left unopened while the people in the beds watched the people who went by with their steps quick and their starched bows bobbing under the lights.

Their faces showed nothing; but someone had seen Father MacGuire on the stairs an hour ago, and he hadn't come through this way; there had been the sound of vehicles at the gates, the murmur of an engine and the slam of doors; and now they were asking: Wouldn't you like the wireless on? It's Music Hall.

They did not want Music Hall. They wanted to lie and wait and listen and look at one another and at the nurses who went by, until it was known, and admitted, and over with.

The sound came suddenly, so long-awaited that it was a surprise, and though the wheels were rubber they sent up a trundling for minutes on end as the trolley went down the drive. The music from the wireless didn't drown it, nor the movement of the nurses as they thumped through the tall swing-doors, fetching and carrying while the sound went on and they pretended not to hear it.

. . . .

In the Town Hall people were jumpy whenever a team came back or a list came in or a telephone rang. There had been no new case for nearly three days. The figure for the Royalty focus had stopped at nineteen when Bradley had been brought in. There had been no more cases from the Cinema, from the Sombrero Café, the Prebble house, the *Gazette* night-office, nor from any isolated source. Bradley had been the last. But at any moment it could start again, because the woman from the Crossings Hotel was still missing and it was almost certain she was infected. Moreover it was quite certain she was a carrier, having been in contact with Bradley during the onset of his symptoms.

They were sitting on top of Buckridge's Bomb and the strain was reflected in their work as shift took over from shift and people refused to go home. They stayed and got in the way and weren't thanked for it.

Just before ten o'clock a call was put through to the main administration room and Dr. Beesdale took it, and in a moment asked for Mr. Sanders' extension, so that those near him turned their heads and stopped what they were doing.

Bennett, chain-smoking in the C.S.I.'s office, waited until Sanders put the receiver down and then asked:

'Is it a new one?'

'No. Bradley's died.' He turned to his clerk. 'See that his name is changed to the proper column in all the lists.'

130

TWELVE

After a telephone call to the Chief Constable a conference was arranged for five o'clock in the afternoon. As Buckridge was in charge of all environmental matters it was to be held in his office. He had sent invitations to the few people whose function qualified them and who were considered useful. Buckridge saw Dr. Tewson personally.

'If Dr. Monks can attend, I think it might be helpful.'

'In what way?'

Buckridge was prepared to be patient. Tewson was a plodder. He accepted nothing from any source outside his own without first analysing every detail. It wasn't that he didn't trust the experts or that he felt that only he could ever be right. It was just his way.

'He's personally interested,' said Buckridge. 'I think he might have ideas, or something might occur to him.'

'It's all rather vague, isn't it, Henry?'

Buckridge took a short cut. 'Is there any reason why he *shouldn't* attend?'

'None at all.'

'Then I won't need to waste your time any more.'

'You needn't have asked me at all.'

Buckridge sidled to the door. 'Well, as a doctor he comes under the Medical Department; but it's nice of you to put it like that.'

When he was gone, Tewson thought for a few minutes about what Buckridge had said. Dr. Monks was 'personally interested'. Now what *precisely* did that mean?

He sent a memo to his people, saying that Dr. Monks was wanted at the conference, so that if anyone saw him in the building they should inform him.

There was no opportunity for Buckridge to talk to Dr. Monks before the others arrived. The Chief Constable came up the main stairs at fifteen seconds to five o'clock, took ten seconds to reach the C.S.I.'s door and another couple of seconds to look at his watch. He was early as usual. He knocked.

Dr. Tewson crossed from his office soon afterwards and found most of them in the room: Superintendent Goffe and his sergeant from B Division Operations, the Chief Constable, the two representatives from the Ministry and its liaison officer, and three of Buckridge's district inspectors. Everyone seemed to be

131

smoking, so Tewson lit up, finding a Stackeasy chair and sitting down. He thought Buckridge looked very nervous.

Notes were being taken. Someone knocked and came in, got a glance from Buckridge and went away, shutting the door as if it were made of egg-shell.

'I expect the situation is known to everyone here,' began Buckridge, 'but in case there are any doubts I'll put it very briefly. The last case of confirmed smallpox was received by King's Hospital three days ago. He was Mr. Bradley and he has unfortunately since died. So far as we can hope to know, all his contacts have been traced and dealt with – except his wife, who is missing.' For a few moments as he went on he stopped the slow radar-finder swing of his head and looked at the things on his desk. He did not like his secret, but until he saw Monks he refused to share it or even let a hint in his eyes be seen. 'Any optimistic hopes that we might now be on top of the epidemic cannot be tolerated until Mrs. Bradley has been found and a list made of her contacts since the time when she abandoned the overturned car on the London road.'

He waited until a bus had gone by and then looked across at the M.O.H. 'Dr. Tewson will be able to tell you very simply the extent of the risk involved while this woman is missing.' He dragged his eyebrows up from his tired face and Tewson shifted in his chair.

'Certainly. Bradley was infected at the Royalty Cinema. His wife might or might not have been infected at the same time. If she was, and if her symptoms develop along the usual lines, she will by now be herself infectious and contagious. In addition, of course, she will be feeling the effects of the illness. Every hospital in the country has been informed of the situation either direct or by public announcement and will contact us immediately Mrs. Bradley is received.'

He was silent for so long that one of the Ministry men put a question and Tewson said: 'I'll answer that in a moment, if I may.'

'I'm sorry, I thought you'd finished——'

'Very nearly.' He disliked Morton, who had been trying to dig at him for a long time about the rap on the knuckles the Ministry had given him for not reporting suspect smallpox after Dr. Monks' diagnosis. 'If Mrs. Bradley was *not* infected at the Royalty Cinema, she wouldn't have been infected by Bradley until about five days ago, prior to or during the onset of his symptoms. Even then we can't be certain she has in fact been infected, but as she shared her husband's bed I would say it's very likely.'

Buckridge looked at his hands as Tewson finished: 'If this woman has not been infected at all, she is still very definitely a

132

carrier, as this disease can be spread by droplet infection in any case. So the point is that even if she escaped infection at the cinema and escaped it at the hotel when Bradley fell ill, she is still capable of spreading smallpox and causing a new outbreak either in this area or in London or wherever she might have gone. This is apart from the danger to herself – which she might not even appreciate despite the publicity we've given the nature of the disease. I'm sorry to have taken so long to explain what must have been prior knowledge to most of you.' He looked across at Buckridge.

'Thank you, Dr. Tewson.' He turned his eyes on the Chief Constable, and then the door opened and Monks came in, and they all looked at him.

'Dr. Monks – I was hoping you'd get my message.'

'Rather late. Am I interrupting?' He looked as if he were emerging from the dark and were trying to remember where he was. Someone swung a chair over for him and he sat down, still looking painfully at Buckridge.

'You're well acquainted with what little we've said up to now.' Buckridge turned again to the Chief Constable. 'Dr. Monks was called out to the case at the Crossings Hotel and found Bradley to have contracted smallpox. As he was the first on the scene with one of my inspectors he might be able to give us even a slender clue to the whereabouts of the woman.'

'I'm sorry.' Steven's voice cut into the room and Buckridge looked back at him.

Steven's eyes were narrowed with the lack of sleep but his stare was adamant, and Buckridge understood. The rest of them were thrown off their balance, and looked back at the C.S.I. for enlightenment.

He made no reference to Steven's interjection. 'We've made sure the situation is understood by those not directly concerned with the main aspects of this epidemic. Now I want to ask Captain Henderson in what way we can help the police in their efforts to find Mrs. Bradley.'

The Chief Constable was watching Steven and said in a moment: 'We would like an accurate description of the woman. The description given us by the people at the hotel is not clear. Did you notice any photograph in the room at the hotel, Dr. Monks, that might have been Mrs. Bradley's?'

'No, Captain.'

'Any clothing that might have been hers?'

'I don't remember.'

'You are working long hours——'

'Yes. And my job is to diagnose. The district sanitary inspector with me has to look after the rest. That is to say the tracing of contacts. Mr. Buckridge could help you there, I imagine.' It was deliberately said and no one doubted it; but they didn't know why.

'I don't quite follow,' the Ministry liaison officer said.

Steven saw no one but Buckridge.

'We are working,' Buckridge explained too casually, 'with very thin material. This woman has to be traced. She's a grave danger to the public and is in a position to kill many people unwittingly as well as herself, by neglect. The people at the Crossings Hotel can't help very much – they're still in their "decant" house and bewildered by the turn of events. I've questioned Mr. Bennett – my inspector who was with Dr. Monks that night – and he has no useful information. This talk was arranged as a matter of policy, but I thought if we had Dr. Monks with us it might prove helpful. He was in the car that was hit by the one Mrs. Bradley was driving, and he afterwards talked to her husband in the room she had shared with him for some few days. He had also taken a look inside the overturned car, where there might have been a clue to why the occupant had decided to run away. But, as Captain Henderson says, Dr. Monks has been working long hours – perhaps longer than many of us – and he is a doctor, not a detective.'

Steven sat forward with his hands loosely in front of him, elbows resting on his knees. He had lit a cigarette that someone had given him. He said nothing in answer to Buckridge. Superintendent Goffe was talking to the Chief Constable, and said in a moment: 'This matter of the telephone-box that was set on fire.'

All their heads turned.

'I understand it was Dr. Tewson who found it blazing.'

'Yes. We put it out.'

'That's right, Doctor. But the general idea seems to be that it was Mrs. Bradley who started the fire. I don't know who first suggested it.'

'It's a theory,' said Buckridge. He had given Steven time to say something and had tried to catch his eye. 'The box isn't far from where Mrs. Bradley was last seen. The theory is that it was she who telephoned the hospital the next day to ask how her husband was. Knowing she might have contaminated the box, it seems possible she set fire to it as a drastic means of disinfection. Normally people don't do these things——'

'They do,' said the Chief Constable. 'They do, believe me.'

'You feel it's a workable theory, Captain?'

'We've worked on worse.'

'In your opinion,' asked Buckridge, 'is Mrs. Bradley alive or dead?'

Steven had looked up. Buckridge noticed the movement. He didn't expect him to reveal anything during the conference, but

134

there had to be this pressure while he was here.

Henderson said: 'Apart from the question of disease, we wouldn't yet conclude she was dead. The mortality-rate among wives running away from their husbands is remarkably low. They tend to run towards someone else at the same time, even if it's only to their mother, and quite often they turn full-circle and all is forgiven. But if that phone-box was set on fire by Mrs. Bradley for the reason suggested, then she knows she's a danger and knows she might become gravely ill herself. So she won't be running *to* anyone, even to her parents; and she hasn't returned to her husband although she knows where to find him and is concerned about his progress – as witness her phone-call to the hospital. This doesn't answer your question, Mr. Buckridge. The trouble is that we've so many other questions on our plate. *Is* the missing woman Mr. Bradley's widow – was she in fact his wife? We don't think so from our experience of similar cases. Was it this woman who telephoned the hospital? We're told she didn't give her name, and the girl at the switchboard says the voice was not familiar to her, nor had she heard the same voice on the telephone within the last three days. Was the phone-kiosk set on fire deliberately, or was it a chance cigarette-end? It has happened.'

He continued to look at Buckridge as he finished: 'The only information we have from the switchboard operator is that a doctor asked her where the call had come from when the unknown woman had rung up.' He turned his head and found Steven watching him. 'She wasn't able to tell him more than that it was a local call from a kiosk.'

The Ministry liaison officer looked from Henderson to Buckridge and then to Dr. Monks. He didn't follow. It was apparent that Monks was being put on a spot by Buckridge and now by Henderson, who was gazing at him with reptilian stillness.

'I don't follow,' he said, but no one answered him.

Nobody spoke, or coughed, or moved in his chair. Sounds came in through the top of the sash window from the street.

A telephone rang somewhere on the same floor, and someone went hurrying down the stairs. There was no sound unfamiliar to Buckridge, so that he was hardly aware of them There seemed to be total silence in this room until he heard himself asking Henderson:

'Did she give you the name of the doctor who made this inquiry?'

'Yes.' Henderson looked away from Steven and shrugged. 'In any case it's a blind alley. You've asked me how you can help us find this woman. I don't think you can. We're working without photographs or a decent description, without any knowledge of the relationship between the man and the woman except the

135

formal entry in the hotel book purporting them to be man and wife, and without any object belonging to the woman to give our tracker dogs. I don't offer this as an excuse but as an indication of our problem. I don't think it's one you can help us with.'

At this point Steven stood up and found his bag.

'In that case,' he said to Buckridge, 'perhaps you'll excuse me.'

The Ministry liaison officer fumed visibly at him. He had to understand what was going on, but it wouldn't look well to protest for a third time that he didn't follow. He would pitch in to some of these people afterwards but in the meantime Monks was on his way out, and for some reason he seemed to be the principal character here.

'Of course, Dr. Monks.' Buckridge didn't show any surprise. 'It was good of you to come along.'

At the door Steven looked directly at Captain Henderson. 'For the record I might mention that during the past three days I've helped in the search for Mrs. Bradley at the expense of sleep, as Superintendent Goffe's men will confirm. I say this to dispel any suggestion that I lack the team spirit.' He went out without glancing at anyone else.

The conference lasted another hour, but Buckridge found Steven in the M.O.H.'s office, drinking cold coffee, when most of the people had gone. Tewson was downstairs still talking to the liaison officer.

'I'm sorry about that,' Steven said, 'but you rather put the heat on.'

'Come back into my room. They've all gone.'

When the door was closed Buckridge said apologetically:

'I was glad when you walked out. It was more than I could handle.'

'Did you make any progress after I'd left?'

'We planned some routine co-ordination. We can't do more until Dr. Preston's been told, and asked if he can help.'

Steven sat forward on the chair, hunched over his hands, and Buckridge wondered whether a doctor knew better than other people when he was reaching the danger point.

'Of course you're right, Buckridge. Preston must be told.'

'He can let the police have something for their dogs – a glove or a shoe——'

'I've been house-breaking again.' He spoke to his hands.

Buckridge jerked his head forward. 'I'm sorry?'

'I hadn't any right to try taking care of his affairs. But I thought that if I did all that he would do – help them try to find her – I could protect him for a time. For once the intent was good.' He squinted up painfully at Buckridge. 'Have you told anyone who Mrs. Bradley is?'

'No. I told the police, before, that it might have been Mrs. Bradley who used the telephone-box, that was all. They were ready to try anything, and started the search.'

One of the telephones rang and he answered it, speaking briefly. When he had finished, Steven said: 'I don't know how Preston's going to take it.' He stared down at his hands.

'We could ask the Press to co-operate . . . tone it down. They needn't say——'

'He won't mind that. There won't be any room for that in his mind.'

'He's got to be told.'

'I'm not backing out.'

'This isn't anything to do with you, remember. You have the idea that it's Dr. Preston's wife we're looking for, and you felt we could find her and put her in good hands without telling him right away. Now we realise we can't. As a friend of his it was generous of you to try to shield him——'

'Generous,' Steven said sharply. 'Yes, I'm always generous to my friends.'

Buckridge watched him uneasily.

'May I have another cigarette?' Buckridge gave him one and said:

'It's my duty officially to tell him, but he's a Catholic, isn't he?'

'He is.'

'Perhaps Father MacGuire could tell him, then. He would be the best. I'm not trying to get out of it. Father MacGuire could give him strength at a time when——'

'I'll tell him myself.' The cigarette tasted foul, but if he stubbed it out he'd want another.

'It won't be easy.'

'That's why.'

Buckridge said gently: 'Let me get hold of Father MacGuire.'

'I should have told Preston before. As soon as I knew. I'll tell him now.' He stood up clumsily. 'Then the dogs can have their glove.'

'It's not only that——'

'By God it's not!'

Buckridge had to answer a telephone again and wrote something on his pad before he put the receiver back. 'A Mrs. Chalmers.'

'I don't know her.'

'She rang from your house. She got on to Dr. Tewson——'

'Oh. My daily woman.'

'Somebody phoned your house and they want to get in touch with you.' He tore the top sheet from his pad. 'Would you please ring this number.'

Steven took the slip. It was a London number he had never

seen before. 'Thank you.'

'Use one of these, if you like.'

'No. You're busy. I'll go downstairs.' He pushed the slip into his pocket, thinking of Clifford's face and eyes. It would be a terrible thing, to tell him.

'Before tomorrow morning,' he said .'All right?'

Buckridge came on to the landing with him. 'If you don't feel up to it, give me a ring, and I'll tell Father MacGuire.'

'Damn Father MacGuire.' He went down the stairs and into one of the hall kiosks. It smelt of stale cigarette-ends and the bulb was yellow with dust. He had to leave it and find some change, and when he finally heard the number being rung for him he wondered for the first time whose it could be. He didn't know many people in London.

A woman answered and he said: 'This is Dr. Steven Monks.'

'Oh.' He picked at the corner of the instruction card over the telephone, thinking of Clifford's face and eyes. 'It's kind of you to ring.' the woman said. He was only vaguely aware of her.

'What can I do for you?'

'I believe you're a friend of Ruth's.'

'Who?'

'Ruth Preston.'

He stopped picking at the card and his voice cleared. 'I know her, yes. Where is she?'

'I don't know. I hoped you could tell me.'

He leaned against the glass panel and began to twist the flex slowly between finger and thumb. 'Do I know your name?'

'Joanna Druten. I've known Ruth for a long time.'

'Yes, I remember.'

'I'm worried.'

'Yes.' It occurred to him she wanted consoling. 'We're trying to find her now.' But she wouldn't know that Ruth was missing. It was Mrs. Bradley who was missing. Or, if she knew. . . . 'When did you last see her?' His speech was quicker again.

'I think I can talk to you in confidence, can't I?'

'You can.'

'You see, she came up to stay with me in town, a fortnight ago.'

'Yes,' he said. This was what he had tried to find out from poor Clifford. 'What happened?'

'While she was here, Clifford telephoned – you know Clifford?'

'Yes.'

'He telephoned and said there was smallpox breaking out in Kingsbourne. Ruth said she'd stay on here until it was safe to go back.' There was a long pause. 'This is in absolute confidence.'

'I don't think any more harm can be done now, but you can have complete confidence in me. Where did she meet this man Bradley?'

'She knew him a few years ago, and then he went back to Ireland. They – only met once or twice. Then he was over here again about two weeks ago and she met him by chance, and they went to the pictures together in Kingsbourne.'

He watched people through the glass panel. They were coming in through the main doors with worn stuffed brief-cases – Buckridge's men. He asked: 'On what day? Do you know?'

'The day before she'd arranged to come up and stay the night here at my flat.'

'Yes, I see. So when she heard about the outbreak she said she'd stay on with you, but in fact took the chance and went back to meet Bradley and stay with him at the Crossings Hotel.'

'How much of this do you already know?'

'It doesn't matter. I know Ruth.'

The footsteps of Buckridge's men faded up the staircase and doors were slamming, above. The light was growing thin and pale beyond the open entrance of the building. There was nothing here to save Clifford or even help him.

Ruth's friend said: 'She told me where she was staying, so that I could cover things for her this end.' Another pause, and then: 'The whole thing's pretty rotten, I suppose.'

'Yes. But necessity drives us a long way. So you realised who "Mrs. Bradley" was, when she was reported missing.'

'Yes. That's why I'm so worried. I rang the Crossings Hotel on Friday and a man said everyone had gone. They were disinfecting the place. I hadn't heard from Ruth and this was before the report about Mrs. Bradley was in the papers. I couldn't ring Clifford.'

'No.'

'Then I remembered her talking about you, sometimes. Steve Monks, a doctor. She didn't say anything particular about you but I got the idea you were an old friend of hers, so I took a chance and looked up your number. I hope you don't mind.'

'She hasn't been in touch with you since she left the Crossings Hotel?'

'Not once. I can't sleep. I feel so hellishly responsible.'

'We have a lot in common. There's nothing you can do.'

'Haven't you any idea where she is?'

'Not really. We'll find her.' He felt emptied at last of the small hope. Joanna Druten couldn't help them.

'Please would you let me know if you hear anything – anything at all?'

He wondered if he would ever meet this woman or whether her name, for as long as he remembered it, would recall only a stuffy phone-box in the Town Hall, Kingsbourne.

'Your three minutes is up, caller. Do you wish for further time?'

'I don't think so.'

'Let me know,' Joanna Druten said quickly. 'You've got my number——'

'Yes. Good-bye.'

They were cut off and he stood in the badly lit box watching the moist imprint of his hand slowly disappearing from the receiver. When it had gone he left the box and took the first few steps towards Clifford Preston.

THIRTEEN

The long dining-hall was almost silent. The lights had been switched on earlier this evening for cheerfulness, but there was a bleakness about those unimaginative white china shades that chilled the eye. Their wan light, reflecting against the hygienic pastel-coloured walls, suggested tea-time on a lowering winter afternoon; but it was spring, and gone seven.

The rissoles were a bad bet. Nearly half of them had gone back to the kitchens, though no one had the illusion that this was the last that would be seen of them.

Outside the building the air was still. The leaves of the laurels down the drive were black and fixed in an iron-work tracery against the fragile sky, and thrushes could be heard a mile away. The light from the dining-room windows – and later from the windows of the wards and corridors – grew warm on the sandstone rockeries as the night closed in, and the colours of aubrietia and candytuft and saxifrage were subtly altered, so that they looked like artificial flowers on a stage where a wind could never blow.

The rumble of buses rolled up from the town and drummed on the big glass doors of the entrance-hall. A copy of today's bulletin was on the green baize board. Of the fourteen cases still under care only five were described as ill and none of them dangerously. Four were satisfactory, two 'doing well' and three convalescing.

Frank Bradley had been the last case, and the last death, for three days. The sound of tyres along the drive brought faces to the windows. This morning there had been a rumour running through the building as quick as a fever – the special ambulance had gone to fetch a case; people had seen it go, and others had heard of a bed ordered for readiness in Women's Isolation. The rumour was not denied officially but died a natural death by middle-day.

If they could get past midnight it would be the fourth day running. But it was four hours to midnight and another seven to morning, and at any hour the hope could be knocked aside. It was the same at Burford Isolation. A coffin had gone out yesterday but there had been no new case to bring in.

Matron's face was no different. She had spent an hour in prayer before bed each night but looked like a sphinx in the staff-room and the wards and had caught Doris Johnson smoking in the store-room and had sent her to the superintendent.

The waiting was difficult. Tiffs blew up as suddenly as dust in a breeze, and ill-temper clattered the knives in the dining-hall. No news was good news, but it got on the nerves. During the long afternoon someone said that one of the cinemas had been opened again, and another report stated that the Army disinfection unit was packing up and preparing to move off. But whether the stories were true or not, they meant very little. A case could come in at any time, opening up a new focus of contamination, and whether a cinema were open or shut wouldn't matter to anyone here.

Father MacGuire had been seen again in the hospital but the trolley was silent. He was here to see if he could help, and to cheer them up, and to talk to Mary. They said she was going into a convent, and felt sorrier for her than ever. Mrs. Monks, the doctor's wife, had spent a lot of time with her. The pretty spring hat had come, with its grotesque veil, and Julie had refused to deceive the girl. 'You look much nicer without it, honestly.'

Mary had looked at the mirror for a long time, sometimes turning it with a cunning movement of her wrist to look at Julie's face and catch the horror on it. But Julie hadn't looked horrified at all. 'With that ridiculous veil it makes people think there's something frightful to hide. You'd be a sham.'

Mary had ripped the veil off and given the hat to Nurse Fortnell; she was a Jamaican and the powder-blue suited her dark skin. She was delighted and got into trouble for walking right through Wingfield Ward with the pretty hat on and then running slap into Sister Gill. The men had whistled and given wolf-calls; it made their day.

'I'm going into a convent anyway,' Mary said. 'I shan't need that sort of thing.'

'You've decided?'

'Yes.' And Julie knew she had really decided, because she didn't ask Julie if she thought she were right.

'I'm glad. Father MacGuire's a wonderful man and it was a brilliant idea.'

Mary looked out of the window and said: 'It's not a brilliant idea, but that's where I'm going.'

Father MacGuire had talked to Julie later in the evening. He had passed her twice in the corridors, not recognising her in the nurse's uniform.

'I never hoped to see you like this,' he said.

'It's camouflage. There's nothing for me to do.'

'I hear you persuaded Mary to give her hat away.'

'No. She just wanted to.'

The drying remnant of the rash was still on her face and she noticed his eyes and said: 'I'm not much of an advertisement for a nurse, but it'll go soon.'

'You were so magnificent,' he said.

'When?'

'When you thought you were dying.'

'Did I chatter? It was the fever. It's odd, but all I remember thinking about was my uncle.'

'Uncle Robert.'

'So I was *talking* about him!'

'He sounded a wonderful man.'

'He was a drunk and a suicide.' She moved her hand. 'But he was a wonderful man, too. I – I want you to know why I said that. It It sounded cruel and cynical. I said it because Uncle Robert was terribly honest, always. It sounds funny for a secret drinker to be honest, but he was. And he'd skin me alive if he heard me gloss over him. People used to say things like 'the Master's not well today – could you call again?' Or they'd say he was out, or 'not feeling himself'. Once he came roaring at the parlour-maid and frightened her silly. He said 'I'm not ill and I'm not out and I'm feeling more like myself than I've ever felt before, because I'm as drunk as a lord and I don't give a damn who knows it!' Now I'm still talking about Uncle Robert – I can't think why.'

'You thought you'd be joining him.'

'In the hereafter? I don't think there is one. I don't say that deliberately to be rude, Father MacGuire.'

'I know. Honesty runs in the family. Don't ever cheat it.'

They had walked as far as the end of the passage and she asked him if there was any news in the town.

'Some people say it's all over,' he said. 'At the Health Department they're crossing their fingers, no more. When will you be leaving here? *Are* you leaving?'

'Oh yes. They won't miss me here, and Steven will, at home.'

'He's very tired.'

'I know.'

'Your homecoming will give him new heart.'

'I think he wants me there. He said so.'

'Aren't you sure?'

In a moment she nodded. 'Yes. I'm just saying it aloud, I suppose. Like looking at a present again.'

'You deserve your happiness.'

There was a door near them and she opened it. He followed her into the yard outside; it was at the back of the building and the light from the windows showed up crates of stores and a group of oxygen cylinders standing like thin huddled men in the shadows.

'I don't think I deserve it, no. But I've had time to think over my sins. I'm going to stop being a paragon.'

143

'Is that what you are?'

'No. I mean I'm going to stop acting like one.'

They could smell the wallflowers on the other side of the yard. 'Do you mind being out here? I've been shut up a long time.'

They walked slowly towards where the flowers grew and she thought of her own garden, and the evening when Steven had said: 'Now the boys have started boarding, we'll shift that see-saw. It'll make room for some roses.'

'All right, Steven.'

They had sat for another hour, listening to the hum of the town, before he had said: 'I was hoping you'd argue, about the see-saw.'

'Argue?'

'Well, I don't think it looks out of place, and roses are the devil to rear.'

She had laughed in the dusk, and before they went into the house he had said suddenly: 'Give you a go?' And they had sat solemnly on each end of the see-saw, going up and down until a sash window had shrieked open in the house next door, and they knew they were being looked at.

It was a month after Ruth had come to her with the strange frightening story, and on that evening she had begun to live again, watching Steven going up and down with his legs dangling like a frog's.

'I was a bad wife,' she told Father MacGuire. 'Now I'm going to be a good one.'

'Have you broken the glad news to Steven?' She couldn't tell in the faint light whether his eyes were amused.

'When we were married, he was going to be another Pasteur. And I was a nurse, then, so I was going to be another Mrs. Pasteur. But he worked too hard to study, and after a long time he said there was quite enough healing to get on with, without trying to set the Thames on fire as well.'

'He didn't say that easily.'

'Oh yes. It was true. He's a magnificent worker, you see, and so he stopped wanting to blaze a trail for his own selfish reasons. But I didn't see it. I thought it was his excuse for being a failure – just another hard-working G.P. with his dreams put away like toys. For a long time I didn't hide what I felt and he had to live with it, and with my resentment that I'd never be a great man's partner or even a specialist nurse in my own right. I must have been pretty insufferable.'

'You must have been very young when you married.'

'Yes. Too young to realise what I had in a man like Steven. I was lucky not to lose him.'

'You must have been a very fine companion. The part of a doctor's wife isn't easy.'

'Oh, I ran things competently, and didn't wink at the man next door – but that's not so important, really. It's——'

'Some think so.'

They stood over the dark velvet flowers. 'You mean to people like Clifford. But they hadn't a chance, those two.' She looked up at him in the gloom suddenly: 'Why is he so *surprised* she does these things?'

'Because they are dreadful things.' There was pain in his voice. 'And he believes there are no dreadful people. He thinks of it as a great sickness. He sees her face as if it were like Mary's. But he can't cure his wife.'

'Poor Clifford, he's so good, and so naïve. His perfection alone must have driven her away.'

The priest was standing still, his big silhouette against the evening sky. She couldn't see his face. 'Mightn't it have inspired her, instead?'

'She wanted treating like a human, because she's weak. He tried to make a saint of her, just as I tried to make a great specialist of Steven. People mustn't try to shape others to their own ideals.'

She remembered Ruth's white face, trying to explain, her voice rough with misery in the room where the apples shone in their bowl ... '*I'm not perfect – I'm not even good ... I'm just me ... and he doesn't know how to help me.*'

Father MacGuire moved against the pale sky.

'You think he should condone her infidelity, and justify it by calling her "human"?'

'Not condone. Try to understand, and then help.'

He was silent, thinking, and in a few moments she had to say without wanting to: 'Hasn't it ever struck you that Clifford might be very dull as a lover?'

The scent of the wallflowers was incongruous in the air.

Without contempt he said: 'For a woman who finds it so important to her, perhaps.'

'I think it's important to everyone, but we tend to hide it in corners.'

'You think broadly, for a woman.'

'Do you know many women, Father?'

As if he had not heard the question he asked: 'Would you condone infidelity in your own marriage partner, then, on the same grounds of human weakness?'

She was looking up at the lighted windows of the building but knew he was watching her. She said: 'That's funny – Clifford asked me that.'

'People often hold views that would change if the subject were brought nearer home.'

She folded her hands across her arms, feeling the damp rising

145

from the ground. 'You must go indoors,' said Father MacGuire.

'I'm not cold.'

A wash of gold light spread suddenly across the grass verges as someone opened the door to the yard.

'Is that Sister Warnford, please?' A nurse was in the oblong of light. Julie called to her.

'No. Nurse Monks.'

The girl's thin shadow hovered at their feet. 'I'm sorry. We're looking for Sister Warnford. Did you know Dr. Monks is here?'

Julie thanked her and said she would be coming in right away. The door swept the light out and Father MacGuire said: 'I mustn't keep you.'

She turned and looked up at him in the gloom. 'Your question wasn't very subtle. It stuck out like a sore thumb. So did Clifford's. I imagine you wouldn't worry the subject if it didn't involve Clifford personally, through his wife.'

Father MacGuire kept silent and did not move. He wondered at the crisp white voice. 'Ruth came to me, nearly three years ago – I don't try to remember dates but it was early summer – and she was in a very bad way. She wanted to die, and I thought it was right to stop her if I could. It took me nearly all night. Steven was in London for lectures. She didn't actually say what had happened, but I knew, and when I asked her, she told me. She'd come to howl on my shoulder and I finished up howling on the mantelpiece – it was a noisy affair and I wonder the neighbours didn't complain. I put her up in the spare room and we could even face each other at breakfast – howling's a tonic, you see.'

Waking that morning there had been an instant of forgetfulness. Dreams had come between the end of that day and the beginning of this, and memory wasn't immediate, so that when it struck at her head in the quiet room she had almost cried out.

'The cure took some weeks. I used to wake in the mornings and look across at him, and when he stirred I shut my eyes because it's a bit like eavesdropping, to watch someone's face when they're asleep.'

There were voices from one of the many windows, sounding down into the gloom, and she looked upwards for a second. 'I don't want you to think she felt suicidal about her little *affaire* with Steven. Her whole life had gone wrong, and that was only an incident.'

He said: 'More than an incident, in yours.'

'At the time, yes. But what did it boil down to really? I'd found out I wasn't utterly indispensable to another human being, that I wasn't in complete possession of him. It was a shock to my ego and an affront to my dignity. I spent days on end thinking about it and torturing myself, and all the time I was thinking about how

146

it affected *me*. In the goodness of time I suddenly remembered that Steven was in this, too! So I begun trying to imagine what it had meant to him, because he didn't do it lightly and there are a dozen reasons why a man takes a woman. I don't know which reason he had. All I realised was that if he wanted Ruth instead of me he'd leave me and go to her. He didn't. He's been just as wonderful to live with since then as he always was before. So I've had eleven years with him, most of them happy, and Ruth has had one night. I didn't know, before, just how greedy a possessive female can be. My cure was complete.'

'It can never be, until he has confessed.'

'Confessed? To me? Why should he? Can't one have one's privacies?'

'You call unfaithfulness a privacy?'

'Unfaithfulness is only a long-winded word for a night on the tiles. There was no cruelty in this – he didn't flaunt her or risk my being hurt because of her. Why should I embarrass him by telling him that I know?'

She thought she heard Father MacGuire sigh. 'And his marriage vows?'

'There were no vows. It was in a registry office. If it had been in a church, with all the solemnity, I should most likely have divorced him for adultery and spent the rest of my life lonely for him.'

'And if it happens again?'

'That's unlikely——'

'It would be more unlikely still if you were to tell him you knew what he did.'

'And make him feel he must tie himself exclusively to me as a means of redeeming himself? It's no basis for marriage, Father.'

He was silent for some moments and she turned towards the door of the year. He took a breath to speak and then they both heard the sound from above them, a voice from one of the windows – and they stood listening for it to come again but there was only the hum of the town in the distance and the splash of water somewhere in the gully of a drain on the far side of the building. Already they wondered if they had heard a voice at all.

'What was it?' the priest asked.

'I don't know' She thought it was a cry of anguish but it was easy to mistake a sound so sudden and not repeated. The nape of her neck crept and she shivered.

'Perhaps nothing.'

'I must go in now,' she said.

'Yes.'

'I've told you this, Father MacGuire, because it worried you. Every word was in confidence, and I've no fear that anyone else will ever know.'

147

'May I tell you what I feel? You are brave and unwise.'

'They usually go together.'

He opened the door for her. The light shone across the healing scars of her face. He said: 'But it took more than a few weeks, didn't it?'

'You're quite right. It took three years, and the shock of this business, and then the long hours when I lay in the bed and tried to make sense of the news that I wasn't going to die after all. In a way it was like being born again. You didn't know me before I came here. If you had, you'd realise how much I've changed in just these few days. And in some way I feel it's partly ... I don't know how to put it without sounding boastful ...'

'You feel it's partly your own doing. You feel victorious.'

'That's it! Victorious – but why?'

' "You have met the enemy, and he is yours." '

The night became black outside the windows except where the lights of the town winked beyond the trees in the park. An hour had gone by and there was no new case. In three hours the fourth day would begin.

They could go down there among the lights again, among the shops – go to the pictures, drink in a pub and be with friends again, if the fourth day came, and led to a fifth, with no new case.

It didn't bear thinking about.

Daisy Fortnell had said there was dancing at the Palais again – she'd heard the music from her dormer window; but no one believed her. There was no holding her now with her new spring hat.

Nurse Monks had been looking for her husband after supper, but no one had seen him, except Doris, and she swore he'd gone up to see the superintendent.

Father MacGuire was talking to Mary again. It was all round the place now – that she was going into a convent. How she'd miss the boys!

They'd heard about Mary's boys.

But you could get on without boys. Look at Matron. Could you ever imagine Matron with a boy, even when she was young? Boys weren't everything.

'It still doesn't surprise me, what she did.'

'What did she do?'

'In the lav.'

'What did she do in the lav.?'

'Didn't you hear?'

There were still tales for the long night.

'Who do they want now, for heaven's sake?'

'Dr. Preston.'

'I should think he's off duty. He's been on since nine this

148

morning. Who wants him?'

'I don't know. Everyone seems to be missing. It's queer.'

Nurse Monks was talking to the young chap in Children's B. He was going on all right but his mother had died a week ago and there was nobody else.

They'd only told him yesterday. The Children's Welfare Officer came up and talked to him. 'Now, sonny, you'll have to be brave.'

'Mum's dead, isn't she?' Just as if he'd known.

Before Nurse Monks had come to talk to him he'd lain there reading an adventure novel, not thinking about his mother. He had said to Nurse Monks: 'She's had a rotten life. She'll be better off now. Now I know she's safe.'

They asked him about his father and he said he hated his father, and that was all they could get out of him. He was going to be discharged in two days' time, but there was nowhere for him to go. His father had gone to Canada six years ago, and now his mother was dead. But all he did was read his book. They didn't understand young Ron.

'When you saw Dr. Monks, did you speak to him, Nancy?'

'No. I just thought I'd tell you he'd come in.'

'You're sure it wasn't someone else, like him?'

'Oh no. I passed him quite close. Can't anyone find him yet?'

'It doesn't matter.'

The trolley-bus wires were flashing like lightning across the dark wide-open windows. The air didn't move. People complained of headaches and said there was a storm coming.

The two porters had a bet on. Ten shillings it was all over this week. If there was no new case before Sunday, Robert would lose his money. You could tell he was a pessimist by the way his moustache drooped.

Someone told Nurse Monks that Dr. Monks was thought to be talking to another doctor in the theatre.

'Sister Maitland heard voices when she went past.'

'But there's no theatre this evening, is there?'

'Oh no. The place ought to be locked, at this time.'

'Did Sister go in?'

'No. She heard they were men's voices, and the only men there would be doctors, or the superintendent. There are no male patients out of their beds and the porters are down in the hall.'

The young brown eyes were bright with the hope of gossip.

'I won't disturb them now.'

The tale went flitting through the corridors.

'She looked queer when I told her. D'you think there's anything up?'

'Why should there be?'

'She looked so queer.'

'You look a bit pasty yourself. Too many rissoles?'

'God, won't I be glad to get out of this place when it's all over . . .'

'What will you do, Doris?'

'You know what I'll do? I'll go to a matinée an' then see it round all over again if it's a good one, an' then I'll go along to the Palais an' finish up at the Monte Carlo coffee-bar. Come with me?'

'I don't think so. I want to go and look at the tulips in the park before they're over.'

'Tulips? You can see them from here!'

'I've seen them from here.'

Julie saw Father MacGuire at the top of the stairs. She was laden with sheets. He stopped when she called out to him.

'Are you going now?' She rested the ball of sheets on the rail of the banister.

'Yes.' He watched her face.

'Have you seen anything of Steven?'

'No. Didn't they say he was here to see you?'

'They said he was here.'

'It would be to see you.'

'Probably. But he seems to have got lost.'

'I don't understand.'

'Before you go, would you please do something for me?'

'Of course.' He helped her steady the sheets.

'Would you just see if they're in the operating-theatre?'

'They?'

'Steven and Clifford.'

His black eyes were alert for the meaning of what she said, but he was puzzled still.

'Is there an operation going on, at this——'

'No.'

'Am I allowed in there?'

'Just knock, and look in. Please.'

'Of course.' He drew the pile of sheets into his big arms. 'Where do these go, first?'

'I can manage them.'

He let her take them from him. 'Where is this place?'

'At the end of this corridor, the floor below. It's marked Theatre One, on the door.'

The trolley-bus wires sent light flickering through the open window.

'Very well.'

She listened to him going down the stairs.

FOURTEEN

The buses had stopped running and the town was quiet. Steven drove slowly from the hospital, and stopped the car outside the Town Hall, meaning to go in and ask if they had work for him. But his nerves were deadened, and he knew he had reached the point where sleep would come over him suddenly and he would drop like a dog. He would be no use to anyone tonight.

Starting the engine again he drove slowly into Rutland Square. A policeman was at the corner, pausing on his beat. Steven lifted his hand to him: it was Riley, who had helped him ease the man out from under the lorry last September. He looked lonely at the corner, standing like another piece of street furniture, a pillar-box, a lamp-post. There were men like him all over the town, standing at corners, pacing, trying the doors while the town slept and left the business of the night to the constables and the night-shift firemen and ambulance-crews, the men at the switchboard in the telephone exchange and the watchmen who sat in their boxes where the road was up, watching their gardens of flickering crimson blooms. These were the pillars of midnight who held the world steady in the dark.

A cat came to the edge of the pavement and sat to watch the car as Steven got out and climbed the steps to his house. There was a note to the milkman in the bottles by the railings, and another to Steven on the hall table, saying that there was a salad in the refrigerator and his shoes had been fetched from the menders. He would thank Mrs. Chalmers for her kindness tomorrow; he had forgotten, this morning, and every morning.

He lay awake. Sleep had been denied for so long that his body now seemed satisfied that it could lie prone in a bed. In the window the half-moon was just clearing the chimneys on the other side of the square; his eyes watched its white silence while his brain kept on spinning, obsessed with the pain of the day; and of all the faces, Clifford's returned most often, the bright lamps of the theatre shining down on his face and hair as he had sat crumpled in the chair with his legs out crooked and his hands beside him, exposing his soft body with the resignation of a man awaiting the rattle of a firing squad, until Steven had wished bitterly that he had said yes to Buckridge: let Father MacGuire do this.

At the time when he had found all the goodness of this man,

151

and had wanted so much to protect him against the inundation, he had been made to do this to him, had made himself do it for no reason he could think of, unless it was that he could ease his own conscience by sharing in Clifford's pain. He had told him, with his breath held as if before the shock of the cold sea: 'Ruth isn't in London. She's somewhere in Kingsbourne. We're all looking for her. You've heard there's a woman missing. It's not Bradley's wife. It's Ruth.'

'I don't understand, exactly.'

Steven told him again, while he screwed himself tight and wouldn't look away. He said after a little time:

'You mean it was Ruth, at the hotel with Bradley? Ruth?'

'Yes.'

'Staying with him? At the hotel?'

'Yes.'

Then Clifford had cried out 'No!' and all his control went. The only words that Steven could hear clearly were 'Not Ruth – not Ruth,' as Clifford moved about to try to rid himself physically of the anguish, twisting his body as if he were struggling free of a serpent that was trying to crush him – 'Not Ruth . . . not Ruth . . .'

In a few minutes he could sit in the tubular-steel chair with his body almost quiet, and Steven took out his cigarettes and lit one sickened to have watched a man in this much torment.

'Then it's all gone. Everything.' Clifford had his hands together, the knuckles blue-white as his hands went on crushing whatever it was between them – the memory of her, or the idea of a future, perhaps the loss of a faith. 'All gone now.'

'We'll find her soon.'

The late call of birds came through the open window, and the scent of wallflowers drifted in on the still air. He put his cigarette out; its filthy taste didn't help any more.

'How long have you known?' Clifford was looking at him, his eyes red behind the glasses.

'Since I brought Bradley in.'

'Why didn't you tell me before?'

'I should have.'

'Why didn't you? Why?'

'There was nothing you could have done, except go and look for her. I've gone to look for her every day and once in the night after the police had gone.'

'Why didn't you tell me?' He couldn't believe not having been told.

'You couldn't have done anything, Clifford.'

'I could have prayed.'

'No harder than you were already, for Ruth.'

Clifford turned in the chair, clinging to it as if it were whirling him through space. 'He never talked about his wife. We wondered, about that. She meant nothing to him.' He swung his head up: 'Did he know who I was? Did he?'

'I don't think so.'

'What have I *done*? Why couldn't I help her more?'

'No one could help her.'

'She said once that she came to me to tap my virtues – wasn't it an odd way of putting it, Steven? To tap my virtues. I knew what she meant. I was sure I could help her. She took our faith, and for a time——'

Catarrh had loosened in his head and he used his handkerchief, hunched over it in the chair while Steven reviled himself for not having told him in the beginning – for not having asked the priest to tell him this. Buckridge was right. The priest could have given him strength. He had denied Clifford the strength of Father MacGuire because he had wanted to share this himself for the sake of his conscience. Was he to wrong Clifford Preston all their lives?

'Does Father MacGuire know about this?'

'No,' said Steven. 'Or he would have told you himself.'

'Not at once – he might have waited till they found her, so that I wouldn't feel——'

He turned in the chair again and was silent for a long time with his face away from Steven, perhaps praying. From the distance the sound of water came in the window, splashing into a drain somewhere. The last pale light was seeping from the sky.

'You look very tired, Steven.' Clifford was watching him from the chair suddenly. 'You people outside are working harder than we are.' All his control was back.

'She met him by chance, Clifford——'

'Yes, yes.'

'It wouldn't have happened if——'

'Yes, it would. She's Ruth.' He got up from the chair. 'Poor old Bradley.'

'Why must you always *pity* the people who——'

'You don't understand, do you? Not pity them? How can you *not* pity them? Do these things make them happy? Was she happy that night, with you?'

'No. She cried.'

'When you scratch an itch, it bleeds.' He put the chair against the wall, very carefully, and the light sparked across its chromium tubing.

'Haven't you ever had an itch, Clifford? Ever?'

'All the time, all the time – there are lice in all our minds——'

'It's an unwholesome act, to you, isn't it?'

'Copulating? With no wish for children? Yes. It's a denial of the source of life. It's murder for pleasure.' He looked at his hands to see if they were steady. 'Thank you for coming to tell me. I'm sorry it was so difficult for you, but you see it was a shock.' He looked down at the glass instrument cases and smiled with his mouth. 'Post-operative shock.'

'I admire your strength.'

'I draw on His.'

He turned the main lights off, leaving only the one above the faucet-bowls. 'I'm not on duty, but there'll be something for me to do. It always helps.'

'The only person I've told is Buckridge, at the Health Department. He hasn't told anyone.'

'You kept it from Julie?'

'Yes.'

'She could have been a comfort to you. It was a lot to have on your mind.'

'I like to keep my own counsel, about some things.'

'One day you'll want to open your heart to some other human. To Julie.'

'You're talking about my meeting with Ruth.'

'Yes.'

'I would have told her long before now if I thought I must. It was two or three years ago. But there'd be no point, Clifford. It would hurt her. I don't think you'll tell her, either. You might. I can't stop you.'

'You could ask me not to.'

'Why should I?'

'For her sake.'

'If you thought it would hurt her, you wouldn't tell her. It's for you to work out, if it's important to you.'

He took out his cigarettes but hesitated, looking down at the crumpled packet and then touching the lever of the waste-bin by the door with his foot and dropping the packet in. 'Buckridge insisted that you should be told about Ruth – that she's really the woman we're looking for – because he feels you can help the police to find her. They want to publish a photograph of her. And you could give them something of hers for the dogs to get a scent from. There'll be a lot of morbid interest. You may decide not to help them.'

'Not help them find Ruth?'

'It won't be very easy for you.'

'You don't *really* think the scandal worries me?'

'Then you must get in touch with them.'

'Steven, why is she hiding?'

'Don't you know?'

'They say she ran away from the hotel.'

'It's because she can't face you.'

Clifford stood with his feet a little apart and his hands hanging

154

down; then slowly they opened, and Steven knew he would never look again at hands as empty as these. His voice was low and bewildered. 'Can't face . . . me?'

Steven turned, hearing a tapping on the doors. He opened one of them.

Father MacGuire said: 'I am sorry. You are still talking.' He looked past Steven to Clifford, who looked up slowly and seemed not to recognise him.

'No,' Steven said, 'we've finished.'

'It was your wife who asked me to come here.' He was still looking steadily at Clifford, trying to learn from his face.

'Julie?' Steven asked.

'Yes.'

'Where is she?'

'On the floor above.'

'I'll go and find her.' He looked back once at Clifford but he had turned away from the doors.

Julie had been putting sheets into one of the big laundry-chutes at the end of the corridor.

'Are you all right, Steven?'

'I'm fine.' Her face was anxious.

'You look dead beat, darling. Is it just tiredness?'

'Yes. I need some sleep.'

'Go home, then.'

'I – had to come here to talk to Clifford. He's got a lot to cope with.'

'Is he all right?'

'I think so. MacGuire's with him. How did you know we were there.'

'People heard your voices. They said it sounded like an argument.'

'No. We were just talking.'

'Go home and sleep, darling.'

'Yes.'

'I'm not a patient any more. You don't have to come and visit me.'

'You'll be home, soon, won't you?'

'If you still want me.'

'It's all I want.'

He had turned back, a moment after leaving her. 'Julie – I phoned the boys today. In their lunch-time. They sent their special love to you.'

'What made you phone them?'

'I haven't, before, have I?'

'They must have been thrilled, Steven.'

'Peter said it was jolly decent of me.'

'Dear Peter.'

'You do want to come home, don't you?'

'It's all I think about. But I'm nervous. We've both changed, a little. It's been a bit of a nightmare, hasn't it?'

Now he watched the moon over the chimneys across the square and thought about Julie, who was not here in the silent room; but she would be, soon. People shouldn't have to nearly die before you could know how much you wanted them. Then Clifford's face was back, staring at him through the glasses and trying to understand, his hands empty at last and Ruth gone from him.

Through the cloud of sleep that was gathering upon Steven, MacGuire said he was sorry, they were still talking, but he was looking at Clifford with his two hands slowly opening in the silence where the instruments glimmered under the glass and the smell of wallflowers was in the air, and the moon thinned between his closing lids, spilling as bright as milk along his face in the night, where so many of them stood in the lonely streets to hold the world steady in the dark.

.   .   .

The telephone was ringing and he lay listening, still not fully awake until cool air moved against his face from the window. He looked at his watch before he went down. It was three o'clock – but in the afternoon or the morning? The house was dark. The morning. He picked up the receiver and sagged with his shoulder against the cold wall and cursed the Health Department.

'Monks. Yes?'

'Hello, Steven.'

The whole room was suddenly distorted and he stood in an odd half-world, saying:

'Ruth . . .'

'Yes——'

'Where are you?'

'It doesn't matter, Steven. It's nice to hear your voice.'

Her speech was slurred and very quiet.

'Ruth, tell me where you are.' He had thought she was dead. 'In your opinion,' Buckridge had asked the Chief Constable, 'is Mrs. Bradley alive or dead?'

'I just wanted to talk to someone. You.'

He had not put the lights on. The window was a pale square with the bright glow of a street-lamp in one corner. If anyone came by he could call to them with his hand over the mouthpiece and ask them to trace this call because he knew she wasn't going to tell him. She was being very Ruth, and sharp memories of her came flicking into him like darts.

'I'd like to talk to you,' he said. 'Tell me where to find you.'

'Dear old boy. I'll miss you.'

It wasn't a call-box this time, unless she had pressed the button

156

before he had answered.

'Ruth, please——'

'Look, I'm feeling rather dreary, and I don't want to talk for long. Because I'm cold. I had to tell someone. Cliff's no use. I thought of you. Tell Julie it was a wrong number. Julie's a darling – Steven? Steven?'

'I'm here. Don't worry. I'm here.'

Her voice lost its sudden dreadful fright.

He watched the window for the shape of a head – Riley's head perhaps, going by on the beat. Someone would have to come.

'Take your time,' he said, to keep her talking.

'It's not much, Steven. I wanted someone to know.'

Her speech was becoming less clear.

'Yes?' he said.

'I loved Brad.'

The bitterness of a lost world was in her voice. He waited, watching the window, but no one went by.

'Yes, Ruth.'

'Frank Bradley. He was the first man I'd ever loved, and he's dead. Even for a bitch like me that wasn't much of a break, was it? Steven——'

'I'm here. Don't worry.'

'Worry? Poor thing, you're out of bed, having to listen to me being dreary. I wanted someone to know. It's a sort of announcement. The engagement notice. With the obit – obitu'rey hot on its heels. You don't mind knowing, do you, Steven?'

'I'm glad you rang me.'

He could throw something at the window and smash it but people wouldn't come for a long time, and then they'd have to get to a telephone and ring the exchange. He willed the blank window to show a head's shape moving across it.

'Ruth, you need help. I'll come alone. Nobody else——'

'It's too late, old boy. I've got a wonderful rash——'

'*Ruth*——'

'Nob'dy can say I'm not fashionable. Steven, I'm a bit tight, because it's lonely here and I'm going to die. You wouldn't begrudge a girl a drink at a time like this, would you? Steven——'

'I'm here. I'll come and help. It could easily be only modified, because——'

'Be your age. I can't face that poor saint again in this life. There's something else I want you to know, Steven. It's going to be a knife, that's all——'

'I wish you hadn't hit that bottle so hard. Why go and wipe it all out just because you're a bit tight and very depressed? Let me——'

'All I want you to know is that it'll be a knife, because when you find me it won't look like that, and I don't want you to think

I had any discomfort. Isn't it a won – a wonderful bedside word – discomfort? It'll look very – discomfortable. Don't let it fool you. Are you there, Steven?'

'Yes——'

'You're a darling, and Julie's an angel. When I told her about us, you know what she said? She——'

'Wait a minute, Ruth——'

'I don't want to stay long here, because it's cold and——'

'You told Julie about us?'

'Didn't she say? Why didn't——'

'When did you tell her, Ruth?'

'Christ! soon after it happened. Years ago. Part of our up-bringing, old boy, while we were all busy growing up——'

'She never told me. That's something I want *you* to know.'

'I said, didn't I? Julie's an angel. You look after her for me.'

The pink cyclamen was on the window-sill, a faint sweet flush in the glow from the street.

'That's all, Steven. You there? Steven——'

'Yes. Yes, I'm here. Do something for me. Give me a chance to help you – I'll come alone and not tell anyone——'

'Sweet of you, but some other time. That wasn't much of a tumble I gave you, Steven, crying half the night – but you said you understood——'

'Yes, Ruth.'

'I'm getting cold, an' it's dark here. Of all – of all the people who made my life worth getting through – you, Steven. You and Julie.'

No one passed the window and he knew it was too late now because she said suddenly after a pause that made her voice strong and arrogant: 'Ruth loves Brad. Oh God, it would've been really something.'

He tried to think of the right words to keep her on the line and his scalp was prickling with sweat and she said very softly:

' 'Bye, Steve.'

The click on the line was final and he pressed the contact down and held it for a second or two and then dialled three nines, and when the exchange answered he said it was urgent that they traced the call. A few seconds ago. He waited.

The cyclamen glowed in the window. Mrs. Chalmers never watered anything, but he had seen to it and the flower burned like a soft pink lamp in the window while he watched it, waiting.

He would need shoes. In the hall, or the bedroom? He didn't remember going to bed. The car was still outside, because he remembered——

'Are you there, caller?'

'Yes.'

'The number was Kingsbourne 30305. The name of the subscriber is Mrs. Oakeley.'

Oakeley . . . Oakeley . . . no . . .

'Address? What's the address?'

'The Crossings Hotel, London Road. If you'd like me to——'

'Police. Police now.'

'I'll put you through.'

Their car would go faster than his.

The glow was against the pines that stood back from the road and its ruddled light flickered across the faces of the people watching. As he pulled up the car one of them turned to him and said:

'It's nothin' grand. Only the summerhouse.'

The light touched the walls of the hotel, and sparks went blowing across in the wind and dying away, and Steven thought this was exactly the way she would choose. All the things she had done in her life, the good things and the terrible, were Ruth.

NEL BESTSELLERS